WOLF, WILLOW, WITCH

THE GIDEON TESTAMENTS BOOK TWO

FREYDÍS MOON

ALSO BY FREYDÍS ☽

Praise For ☽

Olivia Waite named *Heart, Haunt, Havoc* a New York Times Best Romance Book of 2023

"Freydís has created something truly exquisite... Reading *Exodus 20:3* feels like a religious experience, leaving you in awe by the end, wishing for more but also entirely satisfied."
—**Harley Laroux** author of *The Dare*

"Eerie as a haunting, biting as the midwinter night, and as tender as the ache of new love, *Heart, Haunt, Havoc* lingers long past the last page."
—**K. M. Enright** author of *Mistress of Lies*

"[*Heart, Haunt, Havoc* is] filled with dark magic, romance, and high stakes, this is a fast-paced read that pulls you through to the dramatic conclusion and doesn't disappoint!"
—**C. M. Rosens** author of *The Crows*

Content Note

Wolf, Willow, Witch contains sensitive material, including but not limited to: sexual content, body horror, animal mutilation, horror, depiction of mania, murder, discussion of sexual abuse, premeditated abuse, and religious abuse, bloody gore, obsessive behavior, drowning, depiction of panic

HE HAD GREEN EYES,
SO I WANTED TO SLEEP WITH HIM—
GREEN EYES FLECKED WITH YELLOW,
DRIED LEAVES ON THE SURFACE OF A POOL-
YOU COULD DROWN IN THOSE EYES, I SAID.
THE FACT OF HIS PULSE,
THE WAY HE PULLED HIS BODY IN, OUT OF SHYNESS OR SHAME OR A
DESIRE NOT TO DISTURB THE AIR AROUND HIM.
EVERYONE COULD SEE THE WAY HIS MUSCLES WORKED,
THE WAY WE LOOK LIKE ANIMALS,
HIS SKIN BARELY KEEPING HIM INSIDE.
I WANTED TO TAKE HIM HOME
AND ROUGH HIM UP AND GET MY HANDS INSIDE HIM, DRIVE MY
BODY INTO HIS LIKE A CRASH TEST CAR.
I WANTED TO BE WANTED AND HE WAS VERY BEAUTIFUL, KISSED
WITH HIS EYES CLOSED, AND ONLY FELT GOOD WHILE MOVING.
YOU COULD DROWN IN THOSE EYES, I SAID,
SO IT'S SUMMER, SO IT'S SUICIDE,
SO WE'RE HELPLESS IN SLEEP AND STRUGGLING
AT THE BOTTOM OF THE POOL.

Richard Siken

CHAPTER ONE

T EHLOR NILSEN CHOMPED ON a reusable straw, searching for tapioca pearls at the bottom of her almost empty cup. The house on Staghorn Way stood before her like a fresh corpse, empty and fucking *basic*. She sucked soggy boba into her mouth and chewed loudly, assessing the renovated porch and stark white shutters. Total new-age Victorian. Straight out of a Magnolia Network special. She half-expected a middle-aged woman wearing designer overalls to burst through the front door and call the house a 'fixer-upper' or 'the perfect project' before twirling around with a paintbrush thrust skyward.

But it was a run-of-the-mill veteran who owned that cookie-cutter house, and Bishop was still cruising through the Bible Belt with their dapper little exorcist, leaving their houseplants thirsty and alone.

Gunnhild, Tehlor's plump, spotted rat, sat on her shoulder, stretching her pink nose toward the door.

"No knives this time, I promise," Tehlor cooed. She toed at the welcome mat with her pointed faux-ballet slippers and pushed it aside, revealing a single key.

The door whined open. She stepped inside, scanning the shadowy staircase and tall ceiling. The last time she'd breached that entrance, she'd captured a handful of displaced ghouls—coaxed into the house by a stubborn demon—and offered their naked power to Níðhöggr. It was impossible to know if the great dragon had accepted her gift, but after she'd completed the ritual, prayed to her gods, and chanted under the full moon, Tehlor woke with an assortment of rose petals strewn across her bed. Someone had smiled upon her, at least.

Power was a borrowed thing. Sometimes the gods soaked her to the bone, and sometimes they left her parched and desperate, scrabbling for a sacrifice that would earn their favor. Flowers weren't her fuckin' jam, to be honest. But they'd been pretty enough.

Gunnhild's tiny claws pushed through her beige blouse and needled her skin. Tehlor kicked the door shut behind her and twirled in place, inhaling a long, deep breath. She'd scraped this place clean of any spirits. Pulled them through the barrier between life, death, and the in-between, and peeled back their lifeforce like overripe fruit. Despite her successful harvest, and Colin Hart's botched, angelic ceremony, a foul presence lingered. She couldn't place the source of the energy—rage nestled in the belly of the house—but she recognized its brutish hum. Knew the shape of a spirit bending upward from the basement, reaching for another vulnerable magician to latch onto. *Like a remora on a barracuda's belly.* She crossed the living room, dragging her finger across the banister.

Each step brought her closer to the peculiarity stewing beneath the floorboards. She tapped the edge of the archway on her way into the kitchen. Set her empty cup down and skipped her coffin-shaped fingernails across the copper kettle on the stove. Hummed as she cradled a philodendron's rubbery leaf and strode through the adjacent sitting room toward a closed door situated at the back of the house. Hidden, almost.

"Well, would you look at that," she cooed and jiggled the doorknob. Locked, of course. Her voice lowered, husky and private in the lonesome house. "What're they hiding, Gunnhild?"

On her shoulder, the rat cleaned her snout.

Tehlor summoned a shred of power. It inched through her veins, seeping into the lines of her palm. Whatever favor the gods had leant her after her sacrifice to Níðhöggr, it was fading. Feeling her magic lessen was annoying. Like a half-assed orgasm. She grasped the doorknob again and twisted, loosening the lock until it snapped open. On a hard tug, the hinges wheezed, and a strong gust tossed her fair hair. Gunnhild settled in the dip where Tehlor's shoulder met her throat and crouched there, sheltering from the unnatural wind.

Death permeated the air. Sweetness like turned buttercream filled her nostrils. She inhaled, sucking in the dust leftover from mishandled magic then turned on the light and descended the staircase. The basement held an unusual chill. Electricity sparked on her skin, dancing across the runes tattooed on her knuckles. *Something has been torn in two.* There'd been a split of some sort. Life had been removed from a thing unused to living, and Tehlor sensed the heaviness of its leftovers heaped somewhere nearby.

She closed her eyes and swayed on her feet, bracing herself with a hand on the back of a ratty recliner. *Death-marked.* She jerked away and gasped. Gunnhild squeaked.

Places held onto pain, items kept the imprint of aggression, walls were watermarked with memories, and that nasty chair had witnessed the departure of a soul. She remembered a corpse slouching there, grayish and gone, and tempered her grin, whirling around, searching for the source.

"Come on... Where are you?" She took Gunnhild from her shoulder and placed her on the cool floor.

Pacing back and forth, Tehlor held her palms face-up, feeling for something, *anything*. She closed her eyes again and swung from left to right. Spread her fingers until they ached. Huffed with frustration when the stagnant energy refused to budge. *Don't be stubborn*. She chewed her bottom lip, bratty and impatient. *Don't be a coward*. But nothing changed, or moved, or manifested until Gunnhild sniffed around the base of the wall. It was then, as her familiar's dainty snout tracked a patch of freshly laid concrete when Tehlor Nilsen noticed the half-assed masonry job hidden behind a linen shelf.

"No fuckin' way," she muttered, sighing the words like a premonition. She glanced at Gunnhild who stood on her back paws and gazed up from the floor. "You thinkin' what I'm thinkin'?"

The rat wiggled her nose and skittered away, climbing atop the recliner to perch on its armrest.

Tehlor had been a ballerina in another life. She'd spun on sore toes in pointe shoes and pretended she might become a bird or a bat. A creature with the means to make falling look graceful. She wasn't as athletic as she used to be, but her adrenaline surged as the shelf toppled over and crashed, splitting the air with a loud *bang*. She reveled in the hard connection of her foot against the wall, how the blow shook her ankle and radiated through her calf, causing her kneecap to shiver. Her legs had carried her through long rehearsals. Endured midnight ice baths. Stayed taut and reliable. Besides her pride, they were her strongest asset. The concrete hadn't cured long enough to sustain much abuse and caved inward on another clumsy kick.

Brick gave way, falling onto the floor and atop a body wrapped in black garbage bags. Rot billowed into the basement. Tehlor gagged and swatted at the air, trying to shoo the smell of bile and decomposition. *Nasty shit*. She slapped her palm over her nose and punched a hole in the bag with her fingernail. The plastic split easily. Beneath it, pale, bloated skin shone yellow and splotchy in the dim lamplight. She tore the plastic until the form became a person, and the person became vaguely familiar. She remembered him differently—angry-eyed and walking in Fenrir's shadow. As a man, he was plain. His straw-like, ashy hair had greyed, and his features were distorted, but she knew him, somehow. Felt the ebb of his lifeforce nudging against the terrestrial plane, searching for a fissure to widen and slip through.

"You're stubborn," she murmured, crouching to stare at him over the edge of the broken brick.

She thought of Fenrir, sacrifice, and godhood, and remembered a fragment of curious lore...

Wolves guarded Valhalla.

Gunnhild gave a terrified chirp, and Tehlor laughed in the dank, grim space.

"Let's see *how* stubborn."

Tehlor had stolen from crematoriums before, but she'd never stolen from a business specializing in beloved pets. Snatching someone's bestie from their front yard wasn't really an option, and the Rainbow Bridge Pet Mortuary was the only place in Gideon where she'd found a fresh body.

Gunnhild rode in the pocket of her knitted cardigan, making uncertain noises as Tehlor hauled a purebred Siberian Husky into Bishop's house. The dead dog wasn't heavy, but its limp limbs and stiff body made maneuvering it through the hall really fuckin' difficult.

Finally, she plopped the blanketed furry body on the basement floor and swatted her palms together, huffing out an accomplished sigh.

"See? Easy," she said to Gunnhild, who climbed into her palm when she offered it. She placed the rat on her shoulder and set her hands on her hips. "Two bodies..." She nodded, glancing at the unearthed man and the canine corpse. She scanned the rest of the materials. "Needle, tube, cauldron..."

Her boline, a white-handled knife, rested in her basket next to bandages, peroxide, alcohol, and a suture kit she'd found on Facebook marketplace. The crescent-shaped boline was beautiful and tactile, but it wasn't practical for the task at hand. She reached into the basket and pulled out a Promaja cleaver, turning the chef's knife over and setting the thick blade flat against her palm.

Ritual came at a cost. Gods demanded payment. Still, Tehlor held fast to selfish hope. She could use an extra power source. *Slave* was too taboo to say out loud, but *assistant* worked. Sort of. A little bit. And to be fair, the goddess of death probably didn't want him anyway—someone cowardly enough to trick his lover into pawning off generational magic—but Tehlor still braced for a bargain. Whomever Bishop had murdered wouldn't be missed, and whomever Colin had exorcised surely wouldn't be slithering out of hell anytime soon.

It would've been wasteful to leave—Landon, Liam, something like that—trapped in purgatory. Not when Tehlor had use for him.

Before she lost her nerve, Tehlor dabbed a bit of menthol beneath her nostrils, arranged the two bodies beside each other, and carefully placed Gunnhild on the back of the recliner.

"Don't look," she said to the rat and carved a line across the man's bloated throat with her boline.

Rituals on television always started with a chant or a blessing, but realistically, witchcraft was a boring, lonesome thing. Especially Norse witchcraft, which tended to be messier than most. After she made the ceremonial cut with her boline, she set the knife down and then fastened her wheat-colored locks into a bun with a scrunchie.

"Hel, be kind," she whispered. Her small palm fit neatly around the handle of the cleaver. "I come to you humble and wanting, my lady, for I am a child of the true gods, and I wish to carry their glory into the new world."

Tehlor brought the blade down hard, severing the man's head from his shoulders in three blows.

"The dishonored are bestowed upon you, but I request a contract. Give passage to this unclean soul. Grant him access to your daughter, and through his servitude, I will bring you greatness."

After the man, the dog came apart easily. She wiped her brow with the back of her hand, and traded the two, setting the dog's head upon the man's shoulders. Sticky fluid stuck to her temples, and she paused to dip her fingers into the sour blood, spreading like a crimson lake across the floor.

"Honor me with a spectral guard selected from your keep." She closed her eyes and dragged her bloody fingertips across her face, leaving red trails from forehead to chin. "Long is the way, long must thou wander."

The words came easily, uttered from a poem-turned-spell she'd learned years ago. *The Ballad of Syipdag*, solemn and ancient, poured from her in longwinded stanzas as she sewed the dog's head into place, and sutured the patches on the man's body where insects had chewed at him.

Power churned inside her. The more she tended to him, and the more blood spilled, the more entranced she became. She hadn't realized the candles she'd arranged around the room had sparked to life until their light sent shadows flickering in the corners. She didn't notice her breath fogging the air until the ghostly chill crept beneath her clothes, nipping at her skin like a winter morning. At one point, she was reciting the poem, and at another, she was breathing hard, blind and overcome, lost in the overlap between Nilfheim and Earth.

"I am your daughter," she whispered, teeth chattering, and traded the cleaver for her boline, pressing its curved mouth to her arm. "And I am loyal. Give unto me the blessing of vorðr."

Tehlor winced and sliced her fair flesh. The small incision gaped. She dropped the knife, pressed her hand over the wound, and flicked her blood onto the man's body, laying claim, calling his spirit back to the host she'd uncovered and reshaped.

Give me power. She hiccupped. Nausea rolled through her. *Give me a warrior.*

Something brutal and unfamiliar opened in her core. Her magic snared it—*him*—and she held on.

"You're mine," she choked out. Blackness tunneled inward, snatching away her consciousness.

Somewhere nearby, Hel whispered, "Be glad."

CHAPTER TWO

Tehlor woke to Gunnhild nosing at her cheek and the Promaja cleaver pointed at her face. She blinked blearily, willing the shape looming above her to sharpen.

Well, I'll be damned.

Pointed white ears rimmed in black fur twitched. The man's newly attached snout curled back in a snarl. She stared into his wolfish eyes—one blue, the other brown—and laughed in her throat, grinning triumphantly.

"You again," he seethed. An animal growl bubbled up and out of him.

"*Me*," she purred. "What's your name?"

He lifted the knife away and crossed his arms. "Lincoln. You're that witch, aren't you? Bishop's friend."

"Sure, I guess. I'm Tehlor Nilsen, your new keeper."

"Careful," he warned.

She laughed again, coughing through it. Whatever power she'd summoned had left her weak, but she knew what she'd done. Recognized the gift Hel had given her. "Go ahead, honey. Try it. Let's see what'chya got—"

Before she'd finished speaking, Lincoln slipped the cleaver beneath her chin and set the blade against her throat, pressing until blood welled beneath it. She flinched, cursing under her breath, and watched the same, small wound open on Lincoln, darkening the place where snowy fur met beige skin.

"See," she whispered, craning into the knife. Her skin stung and her eyes welled. "I hold your leash now, Lincoln." Her tongue clipped his name like scissors. "Slit my throat, slit yours, too. Kill me, kill yourself."

Lincoln narrowed his eyes and reached for his neck. The moment his fingers found fur, he paused, tilting his head curiously. Realization tightened the muscles in his forearms. She watched him feel across his new face and saw the exact moment shock dissolved into fury.

"Oh, right, that." Tehlor flashed another crooked smile and knocked the cleaver away. It dangled limply from his hand. She sat up on her elbows, blowing a piece of hair out of her face. "You rocked the anthro-chic look, so—"

This time, Lincoln placed his dirty boot on her sternum and shoved her hard against the floor. The back of her head cracked the concrete and she hissed, shooing Gunnhild before the rat got hurt, too. *Motherfucker*. If she could've, she would've summoned a necrotic spell and unstitched his filthy skin. Left the reformed tissue raw and blackened. But she was tapped out when it came to magic. The only thing she could do was sputter out, "Wait, wait, okay, let me fuckin' explain. Jesus, man. Relax!"

"*Relax?*"

"You're alive, aren't you?" She wrapped her hands around his ankle. It was no use trying to dislodge him. He was bigger than her. Stronger. Meaner, maybe. "Hel would've never let you go, all right? I needed to reshape you in the image of a god. You had no problem walking in

Fenrir's shadow when a demon put a collar on you. Why is this any different?"

"Because I had a say in that," he growled, and pressed harder on her ribcage, digging his heel into her paisley blouse.

"Fair enough, here's your..." She strained through a breath and smacked his shin. "Here's your choice: live or die." She paused, meeting his dual-colored eyes. "*Again*. It'd be the fourth time, right?"

"Third," he said, dragging his gaze from her face to where her lean legs uselessly kicked. He eased up but kept his boot firmly planted, trapping her.

She hadn't paid attention to his military ensemble until right then. He was dapper in his jacket and tailored pants, sewed together by a mortician paid to manicure him for a pretty casket. Fresh blood trickled from the wound on his neck, forming a tiny river atop the crusted mess beneath his unbuttoned dress shirt. She squirmed then went limp. It wasn't worth the hassle to fight, and she was exhausted.

"How'd Bishop kill you anyway?" she asked, sighing

Lincoln licked his pointed teeth. "Put a knife in me while we were in bed."

"Brutal."

"Yeah." His voice softened. He ran his thumb along the gold band circling his ring finger. "Then they fucked an exorcist in the house we bought together and helped him put me in the wall."

"Sounds rough."

"Why'd you bring me back?"

"Get your shoe off me and I'll tell you." She lifted an eyebrow. Gunnhild squeaked insistently, inching toward Tehlor's hand. When Lincoln glanced at her, Tehlor added, "Gunnhild, Lincoln. Lincoln, my familiar, Gunnhild. Touch her and *I'll* put you in the wall."

Lincoln removed his boot and stepped backward. When Tehlor extended her hand, asking for help, he ignored her.

"Fine," she snapped, pushing to her feet. She brushed dust from her clothes and analyzed the cut on her arm. It'd started to scab. Stitches would be a pain in the ass. "I needed access to more power, so I used a Norse necromancy ritual to attach your soul to the body you're currently using. You're a witch, right?" She leveled him with a tired glance. "Occult practitioner? Demonologist? Wizard? C'mon, throw me a bone."

"Sorcerer," Lincoln corrected.

Tehlor barked out a laugh. "Sure, whatever. You found a way to use magic. I'm a Völva, as you know, and to conjure more power I needed another conduit."

"Because you aren't enough?"

"No one is enough," she spat, shooting him a poisonous glare. "I brought you back to be my vorðr."

Lincoln cocked his head.

She rolled her eyes. "My guard. If I run out of juice, you'll be my battery."

"Is that right?"

"It could be fun, you know. Hunting for magic, digging up power, pleasing the gods. You don't have to be a sourpuss about it."

"You're a sick little witch." He glanced around the basement and paused at the sight of his bloody skull lying next to the dead dog. "And I'm guessing you expect to hunt for magic in public, right?" He ran his hand over his head, smoothing his ears down. "Explain how that'll work."

"I'll cook up a cloaking spell," she assured. She picked Gunnhild up.

Tehlor hadn't expected to succeed. Not really. She'd anticipated another grubby ritual and rose petals on her bed again. Being placated by her gods. Told to wait, to be patient. But this time, she'd accomplished exactly what she'd set out to do. Her victory stood before her, twitching his cute ass ears, wiggling his puppy nose, alive and formidable. She fought the urge to boop him.

Thank you, she prayed. *For the devout receive and blessed are the fruitful.*

"Am I undead?" Lincoln asked.

"Sort of. Everything should start working again soon. Heart, bowels, circulation." Her self-control evaporated and she lifted her finger, tapping the tip of his snout. He snapped his teeth. Her pinky skimmed his jaw as she jerked away.

"And the organs I'm missing?"

"Give it time, they'll regrow."

Lincoln's disbelief was palpable. He held the cleaver in one hand while the other fiddled restlessly. Blood soaked his upper half, causing his clothes to stick to him, but strangely enough, it was his expression that gave him away, ebbing from anger into fear. His eyes lost their hard luster, and his ears shifted downward. He looked lost, almost. Stranded in a place he couldn't seem to leave. He shifted his gaze to the ceiling and made for the staircase, stepping over the headless carcass on his way.

"I need a shower," he said, tossing the statement nonchalantly over his shoulder. He jutted his chin at the massacre spanning the basement. "Clean that shit up."

Arguing would get her nowhere. She nodded, offering a coy smile. "Where does Bishop keep the bleach?"

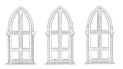

The morning stayed dark, sheltered by mountainous terrain and a fresh dusting of snow.

Tehlor scrubbed the basement, soaked the floor with bleach, righted the wire shelf, then returned the headless dog to the pet mortuary, wrapping the body in the blanket she'd found it with. Her wool coat concealed her bloodied clothes, but red still flecked the blonde wisps that'd escaped her bun, and her knuckles were chapped from harsh chemicals. Snow crunched beneath her boots as she crossed the parking lot and slipped into her old Ram truck, pondering what came next.

She'd done it. She'd reached into the underworld and yanked a soul from the edge of an impossible cliff. She'd asked a god for an audience and received one. She'd found a guard and had no idea what to do with him now that she had him.

"Take him home, I guess," she murmured to Gunnhild who lay on the dashboard, watching tall trees rush by in a blur. "I mean, what else am I supposed to do?"

Gunnhild stayed silent, as she always did.

Like most witches who weren't *woo-woo, spiritual advisor, love and light* bullshitters, Tehlor had been alone for most of her adult life. She didn't follow famous tarot readers on Instagram or tune in for witchy live streams on TikTok. She practiced on her own, put in hours at

Moon Strike Nursery to pay her bills, and sniffed out opportunities to harvest power whenever she could. Sometimes she snipped fingers from cold bodies stashed at low-security morgues or attended full moon bonfires to suck spare energy out of white women who called themselves shamans. She trapped ghouls and ghosts in jars. Fucked occult fanboys and Satanic girlies, harnessing something small and vital and animal made with someone else.

For years, her life had been defined by parlor tricks and thievery. But not anymore. She'd raised the dead. She'd pleased the gods. Tehlor had done something monumental. She was a Völva, truly, finally.

And now she didn't know what the fuck to do with Lincoln.

Tehlor turned on the heater and hit the gas, cruising through the snowy streets toward Bishop's house. She gripped the steering wheel hard. With a viable power source at her side, she could attempt summoning spells and longevity rituals. Unfasten the energy inside another person and take it for herself. Extend her life. Remake herself in the image of the seers of old.

Those who never died. Those who communed with the gods, and the Valkyrie, and the Ljosalfar.

She exhaled a shaky breath. Excitement curled tightly at the base of her spine.

The sun inched over distant peaks as Tehlor unlocked the front door and walked inside, greeted by the sound of violent retching. She leaned her hip against the banister at the bottom of the staircase, listening to Lincoln catch his breath upstairs.

"You're purging embalming fluid," she hollered. "Congratulations, you're officially alive."

"This is fucking awful." His soupy voice carried from the second floor. He sniffled, coughed, dry-heaved.

"Anything left in the tank?"

"Go to hell."

She picked at her thumbnail. "Look, I can leave you here and go to my apartment, or you can come with me. But I'll need access to your blood to make the cloaking spell."

"You didn't keep any?"

"*Fresh* blood," she clarified and rolled her eyes. "I have a shift at the nursery today, too, so figure it out, in like..." She checked her phone. "Ten minutes."

Something rustled. Footsteps came and went, the toilet flushed, and a door whined open. When Lincoln appeared, he scratched behind his ear, dressed in his dirty burial pants, and a tight long-sleeved shirt. He descended the staircase carrying a camo duffel and cast a suspicious glance around the foyer.

"I'll need clothes. Bishop tossed most of my shit." He sniffed the air, dropping his gaze to Tehlor. "But they kept some books—" He jostled the bag. "—and my coat, at least." He traded the duffel from one hand to the other and shrugged on the knee-length garment. High-collared and fixed with polished buttons, the charcoal coat accentuated his inhuman features, turning him avant-garde and beautiful.

Interesting, she thought, and tugged at the thick lapel, *how caterpillars become butterflies.*

"I'm guessing you're not a Martínez anymore," she said.

"Stone." He straightened his shoulders and nodded toward the door. "Are we done here?"

Good name. She nodded and stepped backward, propping the door with her foot. "After you."

Lincoln hesitated on the porch. He lowered his ears submissively and toed at the powdery snow. Tehlor cradled Gunnhild beneath her chin, watching the wolf-man inch forward, placing his boot firmly on one step, another, then the ground. The way he breathed—deeply, slowly—reminded her of beasts at a zoo. Predators in comfy cages, unused to wilderness.

In the car, Lincoln shrank in the passenger's seat, clutching his duffel against his chest. He stared straight through the windshield. Tehlor tried not to look at him, but she snuck quick glances as they idled at stoplights, appreciating his jutting profile.

"How old are you?" he asked.

Tehlor drummed her hands on the steering wheel. "Twenty-six. You?"

His furry brow knitted. "Thirty."

"Thought you were younger."

He hummed slyly and turned to look at her, resting his cheek on the seat. "Figured you were older."

She rolled her eyes. "Where'd you rank in the, you know, red, white, and blood-sport gig?"

"Low enough not to matter. Do you live in the forest with a bunch of old crones, deboning deer and boiling bats?"

She snorted. "I rent a townhouse two miles away. Did you deserve it?"

Silence. She reveled in discomfort. Loved the way a simple question could unmake a conversation. Polite niceties had never been her strong suit, but she'd always appreciated candor. Even when it was dangerous.

"Deserve what?" he asked, turning back toward the windshield.

"What Bishop did to you."

Lincoln was quiet for a long time. Gunnhild's little hands scrabbled on the dashboard, and Tehlor tried to level her breathing, to become unnoticeable. After her pulse quickened, and her knuckles whitened on the steering wheel, Lincoln finally sighed.

"Maybe." His voice was coarse and heavy. He cleared whatever gummed his throat. "Probably, yeah. From their perspective."

"What's *your* perspective?" she tested.

"I thought we were in it together, I guess. In it for the power, for each other, 'til the end."

Strange, how he placed *power* before *each other*. She understood the sentiment, though. Viscerally.

"What about you, Tehlor? You the bad guy in anyone's story?" he asked, smoothly, laughing.

"Most likely." She parked in the driveway and unclicked her seatbelt, thinking about Maggie, the girl she'd sliced open with her boline, and Xenith, the person she'd dated because they collected ancient tomes and she'd wanted to steal one. She thought about the girl she'd kissed in high school, too. The lead in Swan Lake—her first taste of revenge. "Yeah, actually," she decided, remembering how Maggie had said *what the fuck is wrong with you* while she bled on Tehlor's bed, and Xenith had asked *who are you* after the memory spell she'd tucked under their pillow had taken effect, and the sound of bone splitting after she'd made a terrible mistake. "I definitely am. C'mon."

A white door and glossy shutters gussied up the ivy-green, rectangular townhouse. Sharing a wall with her neighbors wasn't ideal, but she didn't mind the kitchen clatter and baby cries every once in a while. As long as the cute transplant couple from California who'd purchased the connecting house continued to ignore her existence, no one would have a problem.

She held the door for Lincoln and swept her arm toward the narrow hallway. "So, I still have to figure out the guest room situation, but for now you can use the pull-out."

Lincoln kicked off his boots and strode into the house. "So, I'm your *guard*, but you weren't expecting me to stay with you?"

I wasn't expecting Hel to listen. She snorted. "It's comfy, pinky swear."

Doors spanned the hall—a laundry room equipped with stacked machines, the first-floor washroom, and a coat closet—and ended at the mouth of an open floorplan. The kitchen was small and boring, and the mustard-yellow couch filled most of the living room. Candles perched on the windowsill and sat close together on the coffee table, and books were crammed on a shelf next to the flatscreen. Gunnhild skittered across the laminate flooring and climbed into her corner hutch, peering at Lincoln from the safety of her bedding.

Anxiety sparked beneath Tehlor's skin. She glanced around the room. Noticed the stale beer bottle on the table and the dishes piled in the sink and hated herself for blushing.

"There's a bathroom with a shower on the second floor. My room is at the far end of the hall, and my stud—" Her tongue tripped over the word. *Studio*. She corrected herself. "The guest room is the first door at the top of the stairs. Feel free to whatever's in the fridge. There's juice and, like, pizza, maybe. It's a few days old."

Lincoln stood in the center of the room, holding his bag and coat, watching her with those cunning, two-toned eyes. "Any chance you've got a pair of sweats I can borrow?"

"I'll check. You good here 'til I get back from the shop?"

"Don't really have a choice, do I?"

She shrugged and made for the stairs. "Take a nap or something. I'll bring take-out home, too."

In her bedroom, Tehlor plastered her back to the closed door and breathed deeply, channeling steadiness.

Okay, well, she'd successfully moved him into her house. She could check that off the fuckin' list. She gnawed her bottom lip and let her eyes slip shut. *You don't even know him*. She cracked her eyes open and stared at her unmade bed. *Bishop killed him for a reason. You have no idea what he's capable of*. It was his ease that unnerved her, though, not his capability. The way he acquiesced, how he leaned in... It didn't make sense. Someone daring enough to integrate with a demon wouldn't be easily subdued, and Lincoln didn't seem to fear much. Especially not her. She tapped her fingernail against her lips.

Tehlor didn't know him. Lincoln didn't know her. They were perfect strangers, and she hoped he assumed the worst: that she was terrible, and wretched, and vicious. She crossed the room and walked into the attached bathroom, setting her palms hard on the vanity. Dark circles purpled her eyes. Exhaustion rattled her.

"Your ancestors conquered the land and the sea," she whispered, staring at her reflection. "You are a daughter of Freya, child of the north, descendent of shield-maidens." She nodded at herself. "Take no shit, bitch."

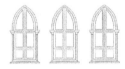

Moon Strike Nursery lived on the outskirts of Gideon, Colorado.

Tehlor entered through the greenhouse, ducking into the warm, balmy climate. Baby monsteras and tall fiddle leaf figs brushed her puffy coat as she passed, and lush philodendrons sent long shadows darting across the floor. Soil perfumed the air. She paused to breathe in the dirt, dew, and pollen and adjusted a grow light strung above a table.

As she walked through the transparent door on the opposite side of the greenhouse, Tehlor swatted the light switch on the wall, illuminating the metaphysical shop. The owner, a grouchy retired online medium, had left a few boxes to unpack and stock, and the tarot table was halfway organized. She rolled her eyes and opened the button on her pocket, gently removing Gunnhild from her coat. She placed the rat on the counter behind the cash-wrap where a snuggle ball—like a dog bed but smaller—sat beside a potted snake plant.

Lincoln probably needs a phone. The thought froze her in place. *And shampoo, and soap, and everything else a person requires to properly person.* She tongued at her cheek. But first, he needed a cloaking charm. She crossed the room and turned on the open sign.

The days usually came and went with Tehlor reading about Viking history, rewatching trashy TV on her laptop, or finding something to clean. Rarely, she'd spend time with a customer, brainstorming the best crystals, deck, candle, or herb for a spiritual ailment. Sometimes she'd recommend an anti-anxiety spell to a baby witch clutching a Hot Topic purse. The last time she'd done anything interesting at work, Bishop and Colin had walked through the door, tiptoeing around each other like teenagers at a school dance.

Funny, how she'd been in Bishop's orbit for a hot minute, selling them plants, candles, and books, but it took an exorcist and a house full of ghouls to solidify their friendship. If she could call it a friendship at all.

She flapped her lips and went to work on the tarot table, and then unpacked the boxes and stocked moon-phase journals on an empty shelf. *Labradorite*, she thought, musing on a stone for Lincoln, *is probably the best option.* Malachite would work, too. She adjusted a few rosemary bundles and turned toward the crystal table, floating her hand above each polished stone and jagged rock.

She grasped one, thumbing at its smooth, flat backing. The labradorite's dark surface flashed purple.

"You'll work," she muttered, giving the jewel a once over.

The bell above the front door jingled. Tehlor closed her hand around the stone and glanced over her shoulder, met with two willowy women dressed in coats, scarves, and spendy yoga pants. One was brunette, the other blonde, both fair-skinned, smiling broadly. The pair cooed at the handmade tapestry clipped beside the door and gestured to the herb satchels and incense in the corner of the room.

"Welcome," Tehlor said.

Of course.

If anyone needed a stark reminder that witchcraft was dictated by Urban Outfitters and Youtube yogis, Tehlor wholeheartedly recommended talking to a white woman wearing workout clothes for twenty seconds. They dropped ass-loads of money on meditation rooms, asked for the perfect prayer beads to take on their all-inclusive vacations to Nepal, and lived in million-dollar cottages in Boulder. Passenger princesses riding in tricked-out adventure vans, drinking spirulina smoothies, practicing breath work, claiming they were *Reiki Masters.*

Tehlor could tolerate curious teenagers and their fascination with spirit boards. She certainly took pity on people desperate for spiritual comfort. But elitist Tesla-driving housewives who crowed about warrior poses and turmeric lattes? Yeah, those customers could choke.

"This place is darling," one of them said, feigning a surprised gasp.

The other didn't look at Tehlor, but blurted, "Do you carry Frankincense?"

Tehlor tilted her head. "We do."

The second woman, the blonde, unzipped her coat, revealing a simple white blouse and a gold crucifix around her neck. She granted

Tehlor a quick glance, flicking her gaze around the red runes tattooed on her knuckles, traveling higher, lingering on the raindrop-shaped tunnels punched through Tehlor's stretched earlobes. The woman raised her eyebrows expectantly.

"You're standing in front of it," Tehlor said.

The brunette gasped again, like a child at an amusement park, and shuffled toward the incense display.

As the pair huddled together in the corner and poked at the shelves, whispering hurriedly, Tehlor took the labradorite to the cash-wrap and calculated her employee discount on her phone. Expensive but doable. She jotted a note on her rolling tab—*lab cab $63*—and placed the jewel in a fabric pouch. She had a setting with a bale and clasp at home. With a bit of honey, blood, cord, and—

"Excuse me."

Tehlor shifted her eyes away from the counter, staring at the two women. Up close, she noticed balm crusted in the corner of the blonde's lips and a cheeky silver bracelet that spelled 'saved' on the brunette's wrist.

"Do you accept community flyers?"

"No," Tehlor said, dragging the word out. Moon Strike Nursery publicly displayed community flyers in the front window, but she scrunched her nose and shook her head anyway. "Why? What's your mission, ladies?"

"We're spreading the word about a joyous event," the brunette exclaimed. Her blue eyes widened, and she smiled.

"Well, I love joy." Laughter flared in her throat. She traded her attention between the two. "Is there a new church in town?"

"Not exactly new," the blonde said, curt and cold. "We're hosting an event next month. Worship, song, praise, healing. You wouldn't be interested, would you?"

Tehlor hummed, considering.

"I'm Amy." The brunette stuck her hand out.

Tehlor glanced at Amy's palm and picked up Gunnhild, wielding the rat like pepper spray. "I'm Tehlor. This is Gunnhild."

Amy jerked away and held her hand tightly to her chest. "Oh my God, *gosh*—well... Well, hello. Aren't you..." She swallowed hard, grimacing. "...cute."

"I have a curious soul," Tehlor teased, lips splitting for a toothy grin. "And we could all use a little healing, right?"

"Some more than others," the blonde said. She hadn't introduced herself, but when she set her credit card on the counter the name stamped on the front said: Rose Whitman.

Tehlor ran the card and handed it back to her. Saccharine sarcasm filled her voice. "Oh, I couldn't agree more."

CHAPTER THREE

L INCOLN BETTER LIKE NOODLES.

Tehlor carried a plastic bag stocked with udon, stir-fry, and tempura into the townhouse. She kicked the front door shut behind her and blew a piece of hair out of her face, tracking snow through the hallway into the living room. She halted in front of the kitchen counter. Lincoln Stone draped across her couch, wearing her ex-boyfriend's old sweats and nothing else. He turned away from a Marvel movie playing on her cheap flatscreen and twitched his snout, sniffing the air.

Half of her hadn't expected him to stay. The other half knew he had nowhere else to go. Her lips quirked.

"Japanese," she said, shaking the bag. "Cheap but good."

He nodded and adjusted on the couch, pulling his feet onto the cushion.

Tehlor fished Gunnhild out of her coat pocket and set her down, then placed the plastic bag on the counter. The labradorite fit snugly in her bra. She kept the stone tucked away as she popped the plastic top off their individual takeout bowls, and let the quiet stretch, waiting for Lincoln to rise from the couch, or ask her something, or make a demand. She'd been awake for too long. Adrenaline ran close to the surface, jostled loose under her chilly skin. She pulled a bottle of sriracha out of the fridge and watched Lincoln stretch his fingers toward Gunnhild, clucking softly at her. Honestly, she wasn't sure if she had the fortitude to wrestle together the spell she'd promised.

I have to try, at least, she thought, warming for a brief, bright second. *We could both use a little normalcy.*

"Food." She nudged a steaming bowl toward him. "You're not, like, vegan, right? Or Keto or whatever?"

"I was dead this morning," he said, matter-of-factly. He stood and crossed the room, snatching a pair of chopsticks from inside the bag.

She lifted a brow and dunked a tempura-fried carrot into her soup. "Fair. Favorite color."

"We're not doin' that." He set his elbows on the counter.

They stared at each other—Lincoln's canine eyes, Tehlor's sleepy gaze—until she tilted her head expectantly.

Finally, he relented. "Black."

"Doesn't count."

"Red."

"Mine's turquoise. Armie Hammer, Ivanka Trump, a wild raccoon. Fuck, marry, kill."

Lincoln chewed slowly. "Fuck Armie Hammer, kill the Trump princess, marry the raccoon."

"*Really?*" Tehlor scoffed, surprised. "The Hammer guy might legitimately try to *eat* you."

"*Try* being the keyword. When did you start practicing?"

Six, she almost said, until she realized he meant magic. "When I was in high school. You?"

"Same, I guess. I didn't take it seriously until I saw it for the first time. Until I met Bishop."

"Makes sense. Think they'll freak out when they find out you're back?"

Lincoln's eyes fell to the counter. He slurped an egg noodle and wormed his chopsticks through the broth, stirring veggies and tender meat. "I doubt they'll stick around long enough to give a shit. The Zach Bagans stand-in they brought home doesn't live here, so..." He trailed off, interrupted by Tehlor's loud laughter. She snorted and giggled, shielding her ugly grin with her palm. He laughed a little, too. "What?"

"Colin," she barked out, cackling. "Zach Bagans stand-in." She sniffled and pointed her chopsticks at him. "I didn't expect you to be funny. You know, with the scowling and growling. Figured you were a hard ass."

"It's not like there's much Bishop can do about it, anyway," Lincoln tested.

Tehlor met his gaze. He didn't look particularly worried, but he was waiting for something. Confirmation. Assurance, maybe. She almost gave it to him. Almost leaned across the counter and snarled *don't worry, honey. You're mine*.

She filled a glass with tap water. "I don't know why they'd waste their time."

"Did you figure out a cloaking spell?"

Her focus narrowed to the stone beneath her blouse. "Yeah. Hope you're a jewelry guy."

"Ring or necklace?"

"Either. Pick."

"Necklace," he said, feeling across the stubborn gold wedding band.

She wanted to ask why he bothered keeping it, but she already knew the answer. It was the same reason she'd built a makeshift studio upstairs. Some past lives were impossible to kill.

"I could make it a collar." She flashed a teasing grin.

Lincoln's snout twitched into a snarl, and he lowered his ears.

She laughed, slurring around another mouthful of tempura. "Kidding, man. Chill out."

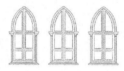

Tehlor set her thumb against the bottom of the labradorite and pressed the jewel into an empty setting, allowing a layer of glue to bond the sterling to the stone. They'd finished eating an hour ago. After Lincoln had collected the trash, he'd asked to see the material she'd chosen for the charm, and she'd thought *well, fuck, might as well get it over with*. Spell work wasn't a chore, per se, but tethering a reality-distorting spell to an inanimate object twelve hours after reanimating a corpse was a lot like mainlining chlorine after a night of cocaine and cheap whiskey. She turned the stone over in her palm, assessing how the leather cord looped through the bale.

"What's next?" Lincoln asked. He loomed behind her, sending hot breath coasting across her cheek.

She batted at the air. "Don't pant on me. I need a bit of your blood, honey, some alcohol, and a..." She paused, glancing around the living room before she twirled and searched the kitchen. She opened a cabinet and pulled a fresh pillar candle from behind some canned soup. "Yeah, this. C'mon."

Lincoln followed her into the small first-floor bathroom. She hadn't realized how broad he was until he propped his shoulder against the doorframe, watching her down the slope of his nose. Like that, with her belly full, and her body begging for sleep, Tehlor lit the wick with an incense match, hit the switch on the wall, and arranged the labradorite necklace around the base of the candle. She opened her palm, asking for his hand.

"Don't freak out," she murmured and lifted his hand to her mouth. When he tried to tug away, she seized his wrist, holding him still. "No tools for transmutation spells. You should know that."

He wiggled his nose. "Get on with it."

Tehlor brought his thumb to her lips and placed the digit between her teeth. A knife would've been easier, but the spell needed to stick, and magic was a bitch, sometimes. If she incorporated her body and used herself as the instrument, then she had a better chance of accomplishing what she'd set out to do.

She held his gaze and bit. He flinched, cursing under his breath. Blood tinged her tongue, coppery and different. Like burnt logs, almost. When she pulled away, warm liquid smeared her bottom lip. Power resembled pheromones; everyone had a unique flavor. But Lincoln motherfuckin' Stone... He tasted *off*. Scarred. Defying death by way of brutality, lust, passion—deep, unyielding *want*—had left him smoky and well-worn.

That taste was a warning.

"See? Easy," she mumbled.

Lincoln huffed. He stood a foot taller than her, breathing slow and deep.

"Face the mirror and picture what you remember of yourself. Hold it in your mind." She guided his bloody fingertip to the face of the stone necklace. "It doesn't have to be an exact memory. You can imagine what you wanted for yourself, what you liked about yourself, but don't get crazy with it, all right? It's a cloaking spell, not a reassembly ritual. You've already been remade twice. We can't keep screwing with your bone structure."

"So, this isn't a permanent fix?" He shifted to stand in front of the mirror, crowding her between the vanity and the wall.

"Carrying a spell around isn't exactly easy, so you'll need to take breaks. Wear the necklace during the day, take it off at night. Ready?"

Lincoln flicked his gaze from Tehlor to his reflection and gave a curt nod.

Tehlor emptied her mind, focusing solely on the mirror. The spell wasn't difficult. It rippled through her like cool water, pulsing from the center of her forehead into each fingertip, delivered with a gentle tap to the face of the labradorite. She lingered in the murky head fog, reaching for any loose ends, chasing out any leftover magic, and swaying on her feet. Her mouth moved around a familiar prayer. *What flies there, what fares there.* She rooted her devotion to the Vanir, speaking strength and steadiness into the scaffolding of the spell.

Her voice was whispery and gentle, gusting from her, "Freya, be gracious." Spoken as a conclusion, sent skidding into the bathroom at the tail end of the ritual's completion.

When she opened her eyes, Lincoln Stone blinked at his shaky reflection. It remained blurry, like the surface of a lake, until Tehlor fastened the chain around his throat. The labradorite rested between his clavicles, and all at once, his wolfish head was replaced by beige skin, tightly cropped ashen hair, and stern eyes—one brown, the other blue—situated above sturdy, handsome cheeks. He felt across his jaw and ear, turning one way then the other.

Tehlor gripped the counter, steadying herself against a bout of dizziness.

"See," she said, sighing, "easy-peasy."

Magic sizzled in the air. She clung to consciousness, watching Lincoln straighten before he shifted his gaze to her. Something eerie and unsettling moved within him. It pushed against the frayed knot her spirit had created when she'd brought him back, tangling themselves into a single, abnormal organism. His gentleness was gone. The guarded, curious guy she'd fished out of Bishop's basement melted into a confident, magically emboldened dickhead. Every woman knew that feeling, the suddenness of becoming prey.

Fuck.

Before she could dart into the hall, Lincoln wrapped his hand around her throat and gripped her by the jaw, slamming her against the wall.

"You fuckin' player," she hissed, scrabbling for his wrist.

He gripped her face with one hand, squeezing hard. "You really thought I'd be your servant? *Please.*" He cooed the last word. His breath ran hot across her mouth. "You're a cocky little witch, I'll give you that."

"I'll skin you alive—"

Laughter boomed through the bathroom. He lifted her higher. She stood on her tiptoes, gasping, trying to summon the smallest bit of magic. None came. She was spent. Her heartbeat quickened and she thrashed in his grip, sending a frustrated noise through gritted teeth.

You knew this would happen, she scolded herself. *You ignored your intuition. You did the fucking thing. Here's your goddamn punishment.*

"No wonder Bishop put you out of your misery," she spat.

Lincoln's triumphant grin fractured but didn't fall. He dug his fingers into her cheeks and leaned closer, fitting his lips against her ear. "We're even, you fucking heretic." Each word stung. Every syllable chewed at her. "You brought me back; I let you live. Come near me again and I'll gut you like a pig. Understood?"

"Taking notes from your ex, huh?" Tehlor met his furious gaze. Rage burned behind her eyes. "You'll regret this."

Lincoln tossed her carelessly. The back of Tehlor's head smacked the wall and she slipped on the tile, smacking her knee against the toilet. She crumbled to the floor and tried to catch her breath. His footsteps thumped in the hallway. Fabric rustled. The front door opened and slammed shut, and the sound of his boots crunching through snow faded.

Motherfucker.

Gunnhild hopped across the living room. The concerned rat nosed at Tehlor's ankle, then her calf, before she crawled onto her thigh and squeaked.

"Yeah, he's an asshole," Tehlor said. She let her eyes slip shut and blew out a breath.

Throbbing pain bloomed at the base of her skull. Magic, depleted. Energy, gone.

Völva slighted by her own vorðr.

She summoned enough strength to scoop Gunnhild up and get to her feet, tracing the candlelight's aura around her ghostly reflection. Slight and bird-boned. Willowy and unrefined. So many people had decided so many things about her over the course of her life. Her dance instructor once told her she moved like a hawk rather than a swan. Too quick; too vicious. An old boyfriend had shaped the word *small* into a compliment. Swooned over her small lips, small breasts, small smile, and small appetite, gift-wrapping each comment as if she'd earned them, even though she'd derived those very same traits simply to please him. A rival ballerina called had her *sweet* once, mistaking her meticulous poise for mousy camaraderie. Witches in silly faux-circles had called her gifted and gentle—an empath, even—as she sat cross-legged at a full-moon party, casing their purses for something to steal.

Many people had decided on Tehlor Nilsen. Crafted a personality for her, assumed her past, predicted her future.

But Lincoln Stone was the first person with enough audacity to trick her.

CHAPTER FOUR

OVER THE COURSE OF three days, a storm barreled down from the mountains and swept through Gideon, quieting into a flurry on the fourth night. Snow heaped atop cars, piled in driveways, and left the town silent. Winter did that, somehow. Crept in, held on.

After a mid-morning snowplow cruised through her neighborhood, Tehlor managed to motor through the empty, icy streets and check on the nursery. The last seventy-two hours had been restorative. She'd slept, soaked in a salt bath, washed her bedsheets, meditated, and held her palm above a burning candle, knowing Lincoln Stone would burn, too.

Magic slithered through her, awake and reinvigorated. After she'd turned on the misters in the greenhouse and shoveled the staircase in front of the shop, she stood behind the counter, dangling a diamond-shaped pendulum above an iPad. A map of Gideon filled the screen. Tehlor held the image of Lincoln in her mind and closed her eyes, waiting for intuition to seep into her fingertips. A spark flared, warming her hand, and the pendulum clattered, landing on Staghorn Way.

"Of fucking course," she mused, shaking out her hand. "Limping back home like a kicked dog."

Pretending she hadn't noticed his power was a balm to her ego, but Tehlor knew what he was capable of. She'd felt it unspool—his dark, deceptive magic—and knew she'd have to rely on wits rather than brute strength to get him back. Even then, there was a high probability she wouldn't succeed. She flattened her palms on the counter and stared at the map.

Hel had given her a gift, granted her a guardian, and Tehlor had been too prideful, or stupid, or ambitious to give a shit about the consequences.

But Lincoln was still her responsibility, whether either of them liked it or not. The gods watched, always, and Tehlor couldn't afford to become another basic bitch in the Nine Worlds.

"*Men*," she snarled, like a curse, shifting her gaze to Gunnhild.

The rat didn't return her sentiment. She lifted onto her haunches and turned toward the door.

The bell jingled. Boots smacked the welcome mat.

Great. Tehlor sighed. She had exactly zero fucks left for the Bible-bangers and their judgment. Thankfully, only one of them walked through the door. The annoying but less prickly one—Amy—grinned and waved, as if they'd been friends for years, and unzipped her knee-length puffy.

"Hi," Amy sang. Her breathy laughter filled the shop. Tehlor resisted flinching. "That incense was ah-may-zing! We'll definite-ly need more for the revival, and—oh, right—I think Rose men-tioned candles. White, if you have them." She paused, plastering on a mock-cringe. "She doesn't know I'm here," Amy whispered as if her box-blonde friend might overhear. "I told her I was going to Hobby

Lobby, but I just couldn't stop thinkin' about this cute little shop, and your cute little mouse—"

"Rat," Tehlor corrected.

"Right! And I thought to myself, Amy, that girl at the moon nursery could probably use our business." She smiled triumphantly.

The world *revival* snuck between Tehlor's ribs. She quirked an eyebrow. "A revival?"

"Oh, yes, our church is expanding, and we have..." Amy paused, eyes lit with passion, or something like it—craze, delirium—and she clucked her tongue, laughing under her breath as she gathered her incense. "Miracles, baptisms, communion, and our midnight mass—" She closed her eyes, swaying on her feet. "—will bring us even closer to God. I just, I can't wait, you know?"

Strange, to hear a millennial wearing designer denim talk about church in a Disney-adult voice. It wasn't Amy's infuriating enthusiasm that piqued Tehlor's interest, but what remained hidden. The undercurrent in every word, movement, and expression hinted at violence. Leaned toward fine-tuned lunacy.

Tehlor rested her elbows on the counter and cradled her chin in her palm. "Totally," she said, matching Amy's enthusiasm. "So, like, what's the big deal with mass, huh? Fancy wine? New worship song? Hot youth group leader?"

Amy shot her a pensive glance. Her lips twitched and she bounced in place, shimmying her shoulders. "I can't say," she said through a whine.

"Oh, c'mon..." Tehlor gave her a once-over. "Isn't a revival meant to bring in new members?"

"Wait, you'll come?" She set her hand against her chest and her blue eyes slipped shut. "Gosh, I knew Rose was wrong about you. I felt it. We met and I said, 'God has a plan for that one.' I just knew, *I knew,*

I had to come back here and see for myself." She crossed the store and placed the incense on the counter, and when her hand closed around Tehlor's palm, Tehlor went rigid. Amy met her flighty gaze. Her voice lowered, secretive and firm. "I swore I saw a light in you."

Freya, give me strength. Tehlor resisted ripping out of her grasp. She forced a smile, nodding curtly. "Of course, I'll come. It's not every day you stumble into a new community, right? I'm a bit…" She wrinkled her nose, wincing like a child. "*Shy*," she lied. "But if there's anything I can do or provide for the celebration…." Her voice trailed off. Tehlor waited, paying mind to Amy's caught breath, her precise concentration.

"Have you ever heard of the Breath of Judas?" Amy whispered.

Tehlor blinked, tempering the urge to startle. Thrill wedged inside her like a splinter.

"No," she lied again. Her own hunger reflected back at her, misshapen and awkward behind Amy's eyes.

Secrets were like botflies, making homes inside little wounds, growing and wriggling, and bursting free entirely new. This one was either true or it wasn't. There was no *maybe*, no *could be*.

Because the Breath of Judas was a powerful relic, and if Amy's church had sniffed it out, Tehlor would simply have to steal it.

Amy darted a glance at the door and clutched Tehlor's hand, squeezing hard. "When Judas Iscariot hung himself, a messenger was sent from the Holy Kingdom to collect his last breath, sealing his soul in a stone vial. Haven found it."

Haven. The church. *Right*. Tehlor nodded again.

Amy rolled her teeth across her bottom lip, laughing in her throat. "Haven is giving birth to Christ's true army. We're going to prosecute the last piece of the man who betrayed our lord and savior." Another squeeze. Fingernails slipped across the back of Tehlor's hand. "I'm so glad we met, Tehlor. So, *so* glad."

Hel's voice echoed from a memory. *Be glad.* And a vicious chill coursed down Tehlor's spine.

The snow thickened and froze, turning the roads slippery overnight.

Tehlor held a glass half-filled with cheap cabernet and paced in her living room. Books littered the couch, opened to pages she'd flagged with color-coded tags. Lime-green for any mention of the Breath of Judas, teal for references of past ownership—San Crisogono, Notre Dame, the fucking Vatican—and pink for passages linked to revivals. She stopped mid-step to flip a page, scanned the information, and then continued stomping.

The Breath of Judas wasn't some bullshit, powerless antiquity. It was a myth in most treasure-hunter circles. A thing people feared and revered—an access point for necromantic magic.

"Look, if the rich lil' weirdo is telling the truth then we have to go to church-babe Bible study or whatever," Tehlor said, flapping her free hand at her side.

Gunnhild perched on the back of the couch, cleaning her ears and snout.

"Because if Haven *does* have the Breath of Judas, and they're planning on destroying it, then they're really stupid or really dangerous. So, we probably shouldn't go alone, right?" She turned toward Gunnhild and drained the glass, exhaling through chalky, bottom-shelf aftertaste. She jutted her hip and exhaled loudly, feeling unfairly judged by her silent familiar. "If I were him, I'd want in on something like this."

But Tehlor knew the truth. Lincoln had power she couldn't access. Power he'd perfected, lost, grappled for, and found again. She might've been the one to facilitate his third whole-ass descent into madness, but that didn't mean she couldn't take advantage of his sorcery. Technically, she had a right to it. She tapped her finger against the glass and hummed, considering. If she tried to track him down in the open, he'd likely sense her. If she went to Bishop's house unannounced, he could very well make good on his promise.

She tapped her foot. Glanced at her phone. Flicked the home screen back and forth. Paused.

Bingo. She grinned, impish and hopeful. *An olive branch.*

Tehlor opened a delivery app, found the cheapest, greasiest breakfast spot in Gideon, and placed an order for the next morning.

The delivery driver arrived at the house on Staghorn Way at eight o'clock. Tehlor had slept a few hours, dressed in a sweater, tweed pants, and a wool coat, and parked across the street, watching. She waited for the driver to set the bag on the welcome mat, ring the doorbell, and descend the porch steps before she got out of her truck and crossed the street. Nerves lit in her stomach. She wrung her hands and took comfort in Gunnhild's warm body in the crook of her neck, hidden by her hair.

The door cracked open.

Tehlor lifted her palms in surrender. "Truce."

A moment passed, the span of two heartbeats, before Lincoln stepped into the light. He wore a crewneck sweatshirt, Target brand jeans, and thick socks, but the normal attire didn't change his two-toned eyes or the richness of his shadow. Darkness thickened like paste, hollowing his handsome bone structure, chasing away the assurance of his humanity. He passed as *almost*, as *maybe*, but anyone with a lick of intuition would sense the chaos nesting in him.

He pushed the paper bag with his toe. "What's this?"

"Breakfast," she said, swallowing hard. "Pancakes, hashbrowns, bacon. Nothin' fancy. Can I come in?"

Lincoln picked up the bag and tilted his head, leveling her with an expectant glare.

She rolled her eyes. "Please."

He stepped into the house and held the door with his shoulder. "What're you doing here?"

Tehlor strode past him into the foyer. She unwrapped the scarf from around her neck, and scraped her fingers through her hair, taming unruly locks. There wasn't much to say besides the truth. She knew that. But the truth was a heavy, unsure thing for two people who didn't trust each other. She hung her scarf and coat in the hall closet, and made her way to the kitchen, fiddling listlessly with the kettle at the sink.

His footsteps brought a memory to the forefront of her mind. *Come near me again and I'll gut you like a pig.* His seething voice; his breath on her ear. He set the bag on the table and took out each container. Like that, in Bishop's big, lonely house, Lincoln seemed misplaced, as if someone had left a child at the wrong home after a playdate. He took plates from the cupboard and gathered silverware from a drawer.

"There's a crazy megachurch in town spreading the gospel," she said.

Lincoln snorted.

"Apparently, they have the Breath of Judas."

A fork clattered on the floor followed by a butter knife. Lincoln stood taut as a statue. He cut his eyes across her, scanning her for signs of a lie. Carefully, he unfastened his necklace and slid the labradorite pendant into his pocket. She'd never seen a cloaking spell come and go so effortlessly. Reality winked, bending until it tore, and came back together more monstrously. He shook out his wolfish head and retrieved the fallen silverware.

"And?" he asked.

She placed the kettle on the stove and lit the burner. "And I want it."

"What does that have to do with me?"

"Look, I get it, okay? You're not my servant, you're not my guard, you're not my friend. Fair. But I'm all you've got." She plucked Gunnhild into her palm and cradled her, stroking the rat's back with one finger.

Anger and fear tangled in her gut. That wasn't the plan—well, she hadn't planned anything, actually—but she'd hoped for grace, maybe. Or the possibility of a shared interest to bridge the chasm between them. When he lifted his chin, staring at her down his snout, she sighed. *Fuck it.*

"What're you doin' here, Lincoln? Playing in your ex's house? Waiting for Bishop to come back with Colin? Really, seriously?"

"Careful," he warned. A growl rumbled in his throat. "You're brave, I'll give you that. But don't push your luck."

"Okay, so, let's talk hypotheticals. They come home, you rip Colin's heart out, and then Bishop hates you for another lifetime. Sure, fine. Or they come home, Bishop kills you—*again*—and Colin yeets you back to hell. Pick your fighter, because I don't see this shit goin' any other way, do you?"

"Or I kill them both." Lincoln shoved a piece of bacon into his mouth.

"You couldn't *kill* Bishop, c'mon."

He licked his teeth. "Get to the point."

"I'm all you've got," she repeated, annunciating each word. "We don't have to be friends, but we should, I don't know, get along."

"Why? Give me three reasons."

"Jesus Christ, man. Why are you like this?" Tehlor snorted, scouring the cupboards for a mug.

Lincoln messily fixed their plates. He sat in one chair and knocked the other with his foot, gesturing for her to sit.

"Marital trauma," he said, smooth as silk. He kept his eyes fixed on his breakfast and shrugged dismissively. "You're really bad at saying sorry, by the way. Like, this is pathetic."

"I raised you from the dead, asshole. And I sent you breakfast *after* you throttled me. If you think I came here to apologize, I'll take my pancakes and go. Hel gave you another life, and whether you like it or not, I was the conduit for your resurrection. We're linked."

"I noticed." He raised his hand, showcasing the blemish in the center of his left palm.

Tehlor flexed her jaw. "Okay, whatever—I'm sorry."

Lincoln didn't seem phased. One ear twitched. He nudged the chair again. "Sit down."

Tehlor brought her steaming mug to the table and sat. She didn't know what came next. Lincoln could plunge a knife into her stomach. He could stay silent. He could bite her in half. She gave him a slow once over, studying the stitches still marring his throat. Despite the predatory gleam in his eyes, he slid a fork through his pancakes, cutting them into bite-sized pieces, and reached for Gunnhild, scratching her with a crooked finger.

"I can take your stitches out while I'm here," she mumbled, picking her pancakes apart with her fingers. She dunked the fluffy pastry into a puddle of maple syrup. "Unless you want to come back to my place."

"Tell me about the megachurch."

She ignored the twinge of annoyance and followed his lead. "It's called Haven. One of their missionaries spilled a few details about a revival they're throwing out in the Gideon Preserve. Fake miracles, bullshit healing gigs, midnight mass, the whole shebang. She told me they have the Breath of Judas, like, in their possession."

"What kind of Christians are we dealing with?"

We. She resisted smiling. "The batshit kind."

"Pentecostal, Catholic, Evangelical, Mormon, c'mon, be specific."

"Shit, I don't know. She mentioned mass. That's Catholic, right?"

He shrugged. "A lot of new age churches take bits and pieces from different practices and make their own thing. Could be the case here."

"Maybe. What do you know about the Breath of Judas?" Tehlor asked.

She gathered some hashbrowns with her fingertips. When Lincoln pushed a fork toward her, she shook her head and kept eating with her hands.

"Someone bottled Judas Iscariot's last breath and sealed it away. Historians speculate it's a source of power—a direct link to purgatory—and could give the user control over the dead. Not necessarily necromancy, but the ability to direct empty vessels. Since Judas took his own life, his breath can't bring back the dead, but repurpose the dead. Corpse magic, I guess."

"So, like, straight zombie movie shit, huh? I'm into it." Tehlor sucked her fingers clean.

"Why?"

"Because we could rob banks," she said, voice smooth as silk. "We could gut the Metropolitan Museum overnight, clean out Cartier and Tiffany's, hell, we could stage *assassinations*." She furrowed her brow, laughing under her breath. "We'd have a never-ending supply of soldiers at our disposal. Soldiers with no fingerprints, no opinions, nothing to lose, and no viable link back to us. That's power, Lincoln. Like, real, tangible power."

"And I'm guessing your intention is to take it for yourself?" Lincoln snorted.

She inhaled a long, deep breath. *Yeah, obviously*. But with his eyes trained on her, and sunlight glowing on the frosty window, Tehlor couldn't decide if her ambition was pointing toward ascendance or self-destruction. The Breath of Judas was Judeo-Christian magic, and her Norse roots weren't known for being merciful when it came to false prophets. But Lincoln Stone, demon aficionado, might be a stronger ally and a more reliable vorðr with it in his toolkit.

"You're the demonologist," she tested, leaning on the back two legs of her chair.

"Oh, so I can pack a heftier punch as your spiritual battery? Cut the shit, witch."

"Okay, look, I... I get it—I made some assumptions, but—"

"Assumptions? Open your phone, Google *enslavement*, and—"

"I'm sorry," she snapped, letting the chair smack the ground again. "You've made your point. Can we move on?"

Lincoln finished the last of his pancakes and held his hand open, allowing Gunnhild to place her front paws on his palm.

"I'm not above killing you," he murmured, shifting his attention to Tehlor.

"You've made that abundantly clear." Nervousness filled her chest. Watching her familiar sniff his wrist, knowing he could squeeze the life out of her, plucked cruelly at her confidence. She swallowed hard. "She's been with me for eight years," Tehlor said, hardly above a whisper. It was an olive branch, that tender information. A peek at her underbelly. "I'm surprised. She's usually shy."

Lincoln stayed quiet. He leaned down, allowing Gunnhild to stretch her nose toward his own.

"Corpses have no free will," he said as if he was mulling over his decision.

"Like I said, you'd have the perfect army at your disposal."

He hummed thoughtfully.

Quiet stretched, filling the house like molasses. The silence stuck to her clothes and caused her skin to tighten, clinging to bone and hope. Tehlor faced the sliding door, tracing their transparent reflection on the glass.

"If you ever put your hands on me again, I'll cut them off," she said, remembering his boot on her chest, his hand around her neck. Her throat went dry. She clenched her teeth until her jaw throbbed. "I'm not saying I didn't deserve it. I did what I did. You did what you did. It's done. Agreed?"

"Agreed," he rumbled.

"Good." She took her rat from his hand and held her close, meeting his inquisitive gaze. "Get your stuff while I put the dishes away. I'm pretty sure there's a service at Haven tonight."

"I never said yes."

She rolled her eyes. "Lincoln Stone, will you pretty please help me infiltrate the LuLaRoe equivalent to Jesus Camp or do I have to find someone else to be my broody spiritual battery?"

Lincoln slowly closed his eyes and heaved a sigh. "You're insufferable."

"I'm aware."

The moment hung between them, strangled and thick, until Lincoln gave a curt nod and stood.

"These itch," he said, pointing to the stitches beneath his chin.

Tehlor smiled and pulled a sleek, black lipstick container from her pocket. She pressed a hidden button on the bottom of the tube and a blade sprouted free. "I got you, boo."

CHAPTER FIVE

H AVEN MET INSIDE A retail space reserved for pop-up markets and seasonal Spirit Halloween stores. Fold-out chairs were arranged in curved rows on either side of a makeshift aisle. The dingy carpet had a nineties vibe reminiscent of old mall culture and Macy's blowout sales, and the harsh overhead lights turned the room clinical and grim. A fine layer of dust covered empty shelves, a janky podium, and outdated speakers. Tehlor loved watching people push Versace sunglasses to the top of their heads, adjust their high-end streetwear, and simultaneously scan the area for unsavory critters. It was like watching dolphins fuck in front of children at the aquarium. No one knew how to explain it, or what to say, if they should say anything at all, but everyone pretended to be comfortable.

"Tehlor, hi!" Amy's voice echoed. A few eyes flicked toward Tehlor, inspecting the newcomer while Amy greeted her with a grin and laid her hand on Tehlor's upper arm. "I'm glad you made it."

Gunnhild squirmed in her coat pocket. Tehlor held her palm over the button. *Stay in there.* "I'm happy to be here. Thank you again for the invitation."

"He will seek out his sheep," she said, nodding. Her gaze drifted sideways. Surprise leaped to her face. "Oh, I didn't know you were bringing your husband. Hi, I'm Amy." She extended her hand to Lincoln as he came to stand beside Tehlor, holding a paper cup filled with steaming coffee. "Welcome to Haven."

Heat blistered in Tehlor's cheeks. She went rigid. Pulled her slack jaw shut and kept her eyes pinned to Amy. *Don't crack.* She forced a smile, laughing to cover a flare of panic, and licked her lips, searching for something to say.

A slow, coy smile tugged at Lincoln's mouth. He shook Amy's hand and then dropped his arm, slipping his fingers across Tehlor's wrist, driving them between her knuckles, linking their hands. "Tehlor told me there was a new church in town. We've been looking for a place to worship for a while now, but you know how it is. Everything's superficial these days."

Amy smiled confidently. Her brunette hair was tied back in a smooth, tight pony, and she'd traded her puffy coat for an oversized turtleneck. At the sound of a polite cough, she turned and met Rose's stern glare.

Tehlor didn't know what to do with Lincoln's hand. She remembered hours ago—his throat bared, snipping thread with her pocketknife, stitches sliding free, a relieved sound blooming behind his teeth—and after that—picking through racks at a thrift store, scouring for button-downs and fitted pants—and watching him descend the staircase in her townhouse, dressed in an eggshell sweater, hard-edged and deceptively welcoming.

"Amy, I see you've found a couple of acolytes," Rose said. Her wheat-colored curls fell around her shoulders. She plucked at the sleeves of her ankle-length dress, adjusting the cool, blue fabric. "Have you two ever been to a worship service?"

Before Tehlor could answer, Lincoln squeezed her hand and said, "Many times. I was raised Catholic and Tehlor grew up Southern Baptist. Like I told Amy, we're hoping to find something real."

Rose nodded. Her sharp eyes transferred from Lincoln to Tehlor. "God provides," she said. Her voice matched her garment, cold and controlled. "Enjoy the service. We'll catch up after."

Tehlor softened, tempering her smile. Her palm went hot in Lincoln's hold. "For sure."

Amy's tight expression relaxed once Rose disappeared through a backdoor. She tipped toward Tehlor and whispered, "Don't mind Rose. Her husband, Pastor Phillip, leads the worship team. She's a bit chilly, I know, but she'll warm up."

"Understood," Tehlor said. She looked around the room, taking in the growing crowd and rising chatter. "What denomination is Haven?"

"Oh, we're Catholic at our core, but we try to be as accessible as possible. Most people who worship at Haven call themselves Christian, spiritual, enlightened—the works," Amy said. She gestured to two empty chairs in the center of the room. "I'll be sitting up front with the worship team, okay? Clear your mind, relax, and have fun. This is a joyful space." She patted Tehlor's shoulder and strode across the room, joining the seasoned members near the podium.

"Well, wifey, there's definitely something weird going on with the blonde," Lincoln murmured. He leaned down, placing a chaste kiss on Tehlor's cheek. Breath coasted her ear. "If we want in on this revival bullshit, you'll have to ditch the bad-bitch persona. You get that, right?"

"Clearly, my devoted husband is the priesthood holder in our house," Tehlor said, saccharine and sarcastic. "I'll take your lead."

"That's a Mormon thing." Laughter chirped in his throat. "Play nice with church Barbie, all right?"

She made an indignant noise, like a snort but shorter, and ignored the rising temperature in her face. *Don't look at him.* But when Lincoln straightened, she granted him a quick glance as he pointed toward the seats with their conjoined hands. They sat. Tehlor unlaced their fingers and reached into her coat pocket. Gunnhild sniffed her knuckles, a comforting flutter on Tehlor's skin, and stayed still as the sermon began.

The worship band played, and everyone stood, singing along. Tehlor didn't know the words, but she smiled pleasantly, attempting to look natural while everyone around her held their palms skyward, swaying and humming.

When the lights dimmed and a projector flashed on the wall behind the podium, she realized just how out of place the Haven congregation must've felt in the hovel they'd rented for their Gideon expansion. The video featured an auditorium filled with churchgoers. A worship band played under neon lights on a platformed stage, and the camera panned from the microphone to a sea of smiling faces.

Okay, so, Haven is a legit batshit megachurch. Tehlor swallowed to wet her throat. She wasn't scared, but she knew what came with sizable territory. Lawsuits, liability, logistics. Haven's website had been intimidating, sure. Being in a room full of devoted attendees? Worse.

When the music ended, the band stepped aside, clearing a path to the podium, and the guitarist leaned close to the microphone.

"We're blessed to be here tonight. Without further ado, Pastor Phillip."

Lincoln placed his hand on the small of Tehlor's back.

"Sit," he whispered. His fingertips skated her spine.

Tehlor couldn't parse the feeling. Vivid heat. Like a needle had wedged itself beneath her belly button. She wanted to snap at him. *Stop touching me.* Wanted to drive a nail through the tender part of her heart that held fast to the false promise of companionship. She couldn't stand how a touch like that, all showmanship, all theater, still managed to disarm her. Especially when it came from Lincoln Stone, who'd used her, manipulated her, and was probably more powerful than her.

She'd always been the upheaval—someone's dreaded Tower card—and this dynamic was entirely new. What a fucked-up thing, realizing she enjoyed the prospect of being overwhelmed. Destroyed, even.

Pastor Phillip grinned as he grasped the microphone and stepped behind the podium. He was young. Mid-forties, maybe. He wore an expensive sweater and designer denim. Sleek glasses perched on the tip of his dainty nose. He looped his finger around the chain attached to his gold crucifix and nodded as he surveyed the room. Each movement was practiced. Every smile, every shift, every breath. All an act.

"Haven," he said, breathing relief into the word, "I can't believe we're here. I mean, I guess I can. It's his plan, after all."

Someone whooped.

"But seriously, let's be real for a second." Phillip gestured to the occupied seats and gave a curt nod. "We knew we'd make it here, didn't we? Some folks back in Austin didn't see the road for what it was, but we did. The path—*his* path—led us to this town, in this state, at this time. And who are we to question that?"

Someone else cheered. Applause rang out. A woman called, "Amen!"

"Amen," Phillip said, agreeing. He leaned on the podium, laughing under his breath. "You know, a portion of our flock didn't think

Gideon was a feasible mission, but no one in this room questioned. We knew Haven needed to expand. We knew God was directing us toward the mountains, toward freedom, toward resurgence. Like the Israelites, we made our way through turmoil and deceit and disbelief, and look around—seriously, look at this place. Is it what we're used to? No. But are the faithful always comfy? Of course not. God's love is huge," he rasped, beating his chest with his palm. "And we are those who listen, those who challenge, those who *know*."

People exclaimed. Amy clapped. Lincoln hummed, an inquisitive noise.

Cult, Tehlor thought. *Crazy fuckin' cult*. She glanced at Lincoln. He tipped his head, as if to say, *I know*, and focused on the pastor.

"We're here. We made it. And in our possession, in our faithful hands, we have something unfathomable. Something only the strong can carry," Phillip said. His light eyes were flighty, landing here and there. He scrubbed a hand over his fair chin. "God is good," he said. The room responded, repeating him in a deep chant. "And with the help of the Holy Spirit, we'll honor him. Right?"

The room erupted. Tehlor folded her palm over Gunnhild, clutching her gently but firmly. The rat nibbled at the skin stretched between her thumb and index finger, attempting to chase away anxiety.

Pastor Phillip laughed again and held his arms open, "*Right?*"

The air was electric. Tehlor glimpsed the stirring of something chaotic, a palpable energy spiraling around the Haven congregation.

These weren't people who'd come to expand.

They weren't missionaries on the path to enlightenment.

As she smiled and clapped, studying body language, expressions, and excitement, she remembered the way starved ballerinas with fractured ankles and busted knees would claw at each other for status and opportunity. Like those dancers, the Haven loyalists had been charged and molded. Recreated to want. To hunger. To believe in the impossible.

Radical hope was a drug like no other. Tehlor knew that better than anyone. And it led to hysteria more often than not.

These are the outliers. She leaned closer to Lincoln, setting her shoulder against his. *These are the extremists.*

"I know," he muttered.

"This weekend, we host our very own revival right here in this snowy, beautiful town. We heal," Phillip said, chewing on the last word. "We mend. We let the spirit move through us, and we don't question." Another laugh. Another burst of applause and cheers. "We're messengers, aren't we? We're warriors. And we're here to make ready *his* house, spread *his* message. God bless, everyone—seriously, thank you—God bless."

Everyone stood. Tehlor did the same, standing close to Lincoln as the churchgoers clasped hands, hugged, and pawed at damp cheeks. *Pussies.* Tehlor wanted to cackle. She wanted to kick over a chair and yell, *are you fuckin' stupid, are you kidding me, you actually believe this bullshit?* But she met Amy's excited gaze and nodded instead.

"The pastor is the ringleader," Lincoln said, feigning a smile as he leaned toward Tehlor. His mouth hovered above her ear. "He's got the keys to the kingdom. I'll introduce myself; you go make good with Barbie."

"Go sit with the other wives and be quiet? Is that what—"

"Welcome to church life, witch-bitch." He nudged her with his elbow and offered a teasing smile before making his way down the aisle toward the podium.

The room hummed with conversation. People gathered in groups or refilled their coffee cups and made small talk. Tehlor overheard someone mention the drive from Texas. Passed a group whispering about the miracles they'd witness at the revival. Smiled politely when someone waved to her. The Norse hawk tattooed on her throat itched. She wanted to hold the charm strung around her neck, a rendition of Mjölnir hidden beneath her blouse, but she kept her hands folded at her waistline and offered a patient smile as Amy turned toward her.

"Did you enjoy the service?" Amy asked. Her enthusiasm was difficult to match.

Still, Tehlor nodded and offered a fake gasp. "You're blessed with an incredible pastor. Is he always so—"

"Moving? Yes, absolutely. The Lord gifted him with charisma."

"Indeed," Tehlor said, pressing the word through a tight smile. She caught movement to her left.

Rose Whitman appeared. She shot Tehlor a cordial smile and gave Amy a hug, sliding glances toward Phillip, Lincoln, and a few other men huddled near the podium. She held a practiced guise Tehlor was well-acquainted with—the pyramid-scheme persona most white women flaunted in Facebook Groups, except much, *much* more dangerous. Rose wasn't selling leggings or essential oils. She was peddling faith. Whatever she said, lie or not, would be swallowed like a prescription.

"Thank you for allowing us to share space with you tonight," Tehlor said to Rose.

She loosened her arms and made a valiant attempt at frailty. She'd been trained to hold her chin high, pull her shoulder blades together, and exude poise. But she hadn't danced in a classical setting for long enough to sag a bit, slackening like a muscle unused to movement.

Rose tipped her head. Her eyes flashed from Tehlor's boots to her face. "You're welcome. How's your heart?"

She let the question rest, considering her answer. *Full* would be too easy a lie to uncover. *Hopeful*, too cheesy. A sliver of the truth surfaced, and she said, "Open, I think." She nodded as if she'd decided on something. "Yeah, tender, too. *Willing* isn't exactly the right word, but it's how I feel. I hope the expansion in Gideon goes well..." She sighed and made a show of gazing at Lincoln. "Haven could be good for us."

"Haven *will* be good for you," Rose said.

Ah, yeah, there it is. Tehlor painted on a grateful smile. *Pride. That's her language.* She'd stroked Rose's ego just enough to earn an invitation back. Or something like an invitation. Assurance, maybe.

"I see your husband's found the boy's club." Rose sighed, trading a Starbucks cup from one hand to the other. Her attention stayed on Lincoln and Phillip, surrounded by other men, but she continued speaking. "I'll be hosting a cookout the night before the revival next week. You should stop by."

"Oh, yes," Amy exclaimed, grinning. "I'm making a keto casserole."

Tehlor almost said *I* and stopped herself. "We'd love that, thank you. Is there anything I can bring?"

"Whatever you'd like," Rose said. Another test. She offered a luke-warm smile. "I'll let Phillip know. He'll send your husband our address."

"Perfect," she said.

Lincoln's gaze snapped to her. He smiled, nodding along to something someone said. His sly eyes hooked around her ribs. Pulled. Cinched everything a little tighter. She wanted to extinguish the fire he lit. Wanted to walk into the ocean and let the waves pummel her, then crawl back onto shore renewed and restored, unchanged and unbothered.

But the spark he'd carried back from hell continued to grow, and Tehlor Nilsen *burned*.

CHAPTER SIX

"**W**HISKEY SOUR," TEHLOR SAID. She hoisted onto a stool at a dive bar on the outskirts of Gideon. It was a small, ugly place that shared a parking lot with a roadside inn and a strip club. No one from Haven would be caught dead in the vicinity. When the bartender asked if she had a liquor preference, she shook her head. "Well is fine, thank you. What do you want?"

Lincoln took the seat beside her. "Whatever IPA you've got."

"You're in Colorado," Tehlor deadpanned.

The bartender nodded solemnly. "Yeah, we have five on tap. Any favorites?"

"Surprise me," Lincoln said. He eyed Tehlor down his straight nose, assessing her in a swift pass from forehead to chin. "What's next?"

She waited for the bartender to leave their drinks and cruise to the other end of the bar before she sighed and said, "The stupid barbeque, I guess."

"Don't you think you should replenish before an outing like that?"

The hair on the back of her neck stood. In all fairness, she should've anticipated his ability to perceive her stunning lack of *umph*. She hadn't fought back when he'd choked her in the bathroom. She hadn't shown any sort of power besides the ritual she'd performed in Bishop's basement, and truthfully, that was more a bargain than a spell, anyway. She sipped her drink and pushed the liquor around in her mouth, coating her gums. A part of her wanted to lie. But the rest of her—the braver, reckless bits—slithered toward the surface, curving her lips into a smile.

"What makes you think I need to?" Tehlor asked. She dipped her finger into her drink and sucked the digit clean.

"You don't seem like the kind of woman who'd take shit lyin' down. Call me a liar, but I think we both know bringing me back took a lot out of you."

Her expression hardened. She snorted, lifting a brow as she drained the rest of her cocktail.

"You're not wrong," she rasped, breathing through the whiskey-burn. "Godhood is transactional. If I give something, my deities will return the favor. Hel gave you back, so." She shrugged. "I could manage a few spells, but nothing fuckin' useful." She really, seriously wanted to stuff her own fist in her mouth. But Lincoln had worn her blood and felt her pain. Even if telling him the truth made her want to puke, enduring her honesty was part of the deal. "I could try to make a blood offering."

Lincoln ran his bottom lip across the edge of his glass, collecting a bit of foam. He was alarmingly attentive. The longer he looked at her, gingerly sipping his beer, elbow propped on the cracked wood, the more inhuman he became. Hellfire still blazed in his mismatched eyes. When his throat flexed around a swallow, Tehlor glanced away from his neck and stared at his hand, then tore her eyes away from that too, and turned toward the shelf behind the bar, reading the labels on each bottle.

Most men bored her. Most men didn't practice demonic sorcery, though. Not seriously, at least. She'd slept with a few who claimed to know power—alt-goth he-bitches who looked the part—but she'd never met a guy whose bite was *actually* worse than his bark, and she hated how quickly she turned into a pathetic simp after finding one.

In a wall, no less. Wrapped in a garbage bag.

Christ, she wanted to kick her own ass.

"A sacrifice? In this economy?" He tapped his pint against her empty glass. "Good luck finding anyone worth a damn."

"*My* blood," she corrected.

Lincoln tilted his head. Muted light scaled his jaw, sending a shadow along the seam where his neck became two pieces. "I've heard your deities accept other forms of worship, too."

"Sex?" Tehlor stole the power of a proposition from him. Took his ability to make her blush or stumble, and mimicked his posture, allowing her head to loll. The whiskey gave her courage. "Yeah, we could fuck. That'd probably do the trick."

The self-proclaimed sorcerer didn't bother with an eyeroll. Instead, a boyish laugh punched out of him, and he furrowed his brow, slack-jawed and struck halfway to a grin. "Well, call me Tucker Carlson, because I must be a fuckin' idiot, but aren't you *gay?*"

"No, men are just easy to scare," she assured, chomping at the air like a gator. "I don't know if anyone would grant me an audience this soon after my last ritual, but I could try. Blood magic might work, sex magic might work—" She winked, shot him a finger-gun, and immediately regretted it. "—but there's no guarantee." Treating the whole thing like a joke was much easier than taking him seriously. "Best bet? Find a low-level witch and syphon some of their energy."

"Wasn't that what you brought me back for?"

She nodded. "Originally, yeah."

"And what would *syphoning* from me look like?"

"I don't know—I've never had a vorðr. A simple transference spell would probably work, though. Nothing too invasive."

Lincoln stayed quiet for a long, strained moment. He stared hard at Tehlor. When he placed his thumb below her chin, touching the red hawk tattooed on her throat, she froze.

"We've come to an understanding, haven't we? I could squeeze the life out of you. Crush your windpipe. Shatter your ribcage." He traced the bird's feathers, following its jagged shape to her shoulder. "You could put me back in the wall. Poison me. Stab me again. Send me straight to hell."

He offered a small smile and met her gaze. *Eyes like the tropics,* she thought. *Easy to drown in.*

"I bet you fuck like a porn star," he added, voice low, hinting at reverence.

Tehlor kept her expression neutral despite the heat roiling in her groin. She leaned closer, sighing softly. "I bet you're into weird shit. *Uwu* and *ara-ara* while you're balls deep, huh?"

Lincoln laughed again, that good, strong laugh. He swept his hand higher, pressing his thumb to her bottom lip. "I like you, witch-bitch. You're brave."

Brave sounded like *careless*.

"No need to lie," she whispered, flashing a grin. "We both know what this is."

"Ritualism?"

"Convenience."

Lincoln furrowed his brow. "Can't argue that."

She leaned away and swatted his hand. Playfully, of course. "You hungry?"

"I could eat."

"We'll grab something on the way home, c'mon," she said.

Tehlor left cash on the bar and tried not to notice Lincoln's palm on her lower back, resting there for a moment, thumb smoothing across her tailbone, before he dropped his hand and kept pace at her side.

Loneliness was a disruptive thing. She knew that all too well.

Still, she felt undone, as if her bones had gone soft and betrayed her.

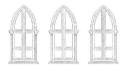

Tehlor upended a paper bag, spilling the rest of her McDonald's fries onto the countertop.

Lincoln searched for liquid at the bottom of his plastic cup, sucking carbonated bubbles through a striped straw.

Well, fuck. She dunked her fries into puddled ketchup and met his eyes, chomping.

"It doesn't have to be sex," he said, so blatantly she bristled. "Intimacy isn't always—"

"You sound like my therapist."

"Well, you look scared shitless."

She rolled her eyes. Anxiety churned her stomach, but she shrugged, attempting to conceal her nerves with a smile. "We'll reconvene in the morning, all right? It's late, I need to shower, you should probably prepare for whatever spell we'll cook up, and—"

"You've got quite a bark, Tehlor. Talk a big game, too."

"I'm not afraid of you, Lincoln," she lied and scooped Gunnhild into her palm. "I'm tired. Fucking you doesn't sound better than sleep, so." She shot him a lazy grin. "We'll get it done in the morning."

Get it done. He silently mouthed each word and raised his brows, nodding slowly. He followed her with his two-toned eyes as she crossed the living room and made for the stairs. She swallowed to wet her throat and worked to conceal the shame brewing hot in her cheeks. *Get it together*, she thought. *What the hell is wrong with you?* But she knew exactly what had gone wrong. It was Lincoln Stone's fault. His power, his charm, his energy, everything about him disarmed her.

Usually, Tehlor prowled around, found someone to have a good time with or syphon power from, and went about her life unbothered. But Lincoln made the prospect of an unremarkable act—sex, coupling—into something delicious. Something she yearned for. Something that eroded the concrete she'd built around her heart and turned her into a blushing schoolgirl.

Tehlor closed her bedroom door and let her weight go heavy against it.

"Stupid," she seethed, whispering under her breath, and banged the back of her head against the wood. "*Stupid.*"

Gunnhild squirmed and nibbled Tehlor's knuckle, asking to be put down. Tehlor set her on the floor and plopped on her rear. She pulled her knees to her chest and hugged her shins. The rat scurried to the dresser, climbed a tiny rope bridge typically strung from corner to corner in metal cages, and curled up in her puffy, circular bed next to the jewelry box. Like always, her bedroom was dimly lit and a fucking *disaster*. Clothes littered the ground. The attached bathroom was wrecked. Lotion bottles, perfumes, an overflowing trash can, and dirty underwear crowded the space. The longer she sat there, looking at her hovel, the more unbearable her nervous energy became.

After a moment of wallowing, Tehlor jolted to her feet and stomped around, filling the laundry basket, tidying the nightstand, scrubbing her bathroom vanity, and fluffing her bedding. It took an hour, maybe longer, before she gave herself permission to stand in the center of her bedroom and look around again.

She exhaled, deflating. *There. Some goddamn control.*

What did the Breath of Judas even look like? How would they get their hands on it? What would happen afterward? Would Lincoln just walk away again? Crawl back to Bishop's house and wait for them to arrive with the not-priest and then, what, kill them, eat them, *what?* What happened once Tehlor didn't need Lincoln and he didn't need her and—

Tehlor had to turn her mind off. She huffed and crossed the room, yanking impatiently on her nightstand drawer. A single pre-rolled joint was all she had left from her last run to the dispensary, but it would do.

She ran a bath. Added caramel salts and a bath-oil melt. Searched through drawers until she found a lighter. Sighed.

Once she'd slipped into the soft water, she lit the joint and closed her eyes, tipping her head against the dip in the tub, exhaling smoky plumes. Her skin stung at first. After she took two long pulls from the joint, her muscles relaxed, and the tension drained from her body. She puffed slowly, holding the smoke in her lungs until they spasmed, and then let it curl from her nose and lips. Her mind drifted. Everything quieted, like static on a television, or rain on a porch. As she soaked, she tried not to focus on a single thing except being alive. It was then, as her eyelashes fluttered and she inhaled deeply, that she felt the knot beneath her navel pull tighter. The touch was ghostly; amorphous. It moved through her in steady waves—pleasure, or something akin to it—and plucked tenderly on her nerves.

Tehlor cracked her eyes open. She paused, holding the joint to her lips, and pushed her thighs together. *Well, fuck*. She swallowed, enduring the creeping incline of heat and pleasure climb inside her. It was like she had her hand between her legs. Like she was teasing herself. *You bastard.*

The connection linking Tehlor and Lincoln protected her from him. Kept him at bay. Forced him to preserve her life in order to keep his own. But it also meant *sharing*. Pain, pleasure, wounds, touch. Tehlor felt him unraveling inside her. His grip, secure and firm, was an internal pressure she couldn't escape. She sighed and set the roach on the side of the tub, chewing hard on her bottom lip. Somewhere downstairs, probably on her fucking couch, Lincoln Stone was getting himself off.

Tehlor wanted to strangle him.

Tension pulled like a string through her center. She was chasing an echo. Running after a ripple on a still lake, unable to reach the source. She couldn't pin down where the pleasure stopped and started. Couldn't access the necessary rhythm that would push her body to a place where climax was accessible. She stared at the white ceiling, watching steam blur the air, breath hitched, skin feverish.

She could endure it, or she could entertain it. Being alone, but not, and seen, but not made the idea of being *with* him easier to swallow. He couldn't see the way her back arched, or how she touched herself beneath the water. He couldn't hear her shredded breath, or judge how her jaw slackened, how her body shuddered. The heat curling inside her knotted and flexed. She felt the strain in him. The resistance. Recognized his gritted teeth, a weight in her own mouth, and the throbbing in his groin, pulsing through her pelvis. She propped her leg on the side of the tub and plunged her fingers deep, widening herself on bony, tattooed knuckles, and imagined it was his hand. She came like that, thinking of him, and felt his orgasm shake through her seconds later. The pressure caused her back to bow. She lurched forward, smacking her free hand over her mouth to silence a shout, and bucked her hips, sending water splashing onto the bathroom floor.

Everything blurred. She caught her breath, staring at the shower-head clipped to the wall, and let her head sink beneath the water. The world went silent except for her heartbeat, drumming in time with his, like war horses. She breached and sucked in a breath, righting herself against the static rippling through her body.

Seconds turned to minutes. Her muscles unclenched and her pulse slowed. The water cooled. Every thought that'd emptied when she'd entered the bath came rushing back, clawing through her cloudy mind—fuzzy from weed and pleasure.

For a long, long time Tehlor had confronted sex and togetherness cautiously or with distinct intent. Never to bond with someone, not to build a life with someone, but for power, control, or information. She used people, but she was never used *by* people. She got what she wanted and went on her way.

Whatever the fuck was going on between her and Lincoln wasn't part of the plan.

Not the short-term plan. Not the long-term plan.

"Get the Breath of Judas. Power him up. Syphon his power. Easy," she whispered and chewed her bottom lip. "Easy-peasy."

Tehlor was a talented liar, but she'd never been very good at lying to herself.

She rose from the bath and stepped out. She didn't bother with a towel, just stomped through her bedroom, threw open the door, and stormed down the hall. Her feet left watermarks on the staircase.

Lincoln lounged with his arm draped over the back of the couch, his wolfish head tipped toward the ceiling, shirtless and relaxed in the center of the sofa. She inhaled sharply and rounded the furniture in the dark living room, and didn't stop when he opened his eyes, startled. She moved efficiently, straddling him in one swift lunge, and seized his face with both hands.

His pointed ears stayed perked, framed by her thumbs. She ran her fingers through his fur and met his eyes. He snarled, confused or surprised, likely both, and went rigid. Water dripped from her nose and her soaked hair plastered to her naked skin. Despite being so, *so* disgustingly enchanted by him, his power, how he looked at her, she was in control, at ease in her body.

Lincoln kept his palms open, hovering an inch above her hips. Afraid she might detonate if he touched her, probably.

Good, she thought. *Be scared, sorcerer.*

"You ever do that to me again, I'll castrate you," she whispered.

Lincoln licked his maw. "I doubt that, witchling."

Witchling. Tehlor set her teeth and dug her fingernails into his skull. If her blush worsened, the water on her skin would turn to steam. She shoved his face away and climbed out of his lap, leaving him damp and alone.

"Goodnight," he called after her.

Tehlor hurried up the stairs and slammed her bedroom door. She twirled a piece of his fur between her fingers and smiled, tucking the strand under her tongue. She focused on Lincoln—two-toned eyes, wide hands, broad chest, wicked smile—and called to Nótt, goddess of night.

Dream of me, she silently chanted, swaying on her feet, *dream of me, dream of me, dream of me.*

"Drive him to madness," she whispered, sighing, and chewed his fur. "Fill his dreamscape with nothing but me. Let my body be a heatwave. I am a ritual. I am a ritual. I am *his* ritual." She imagined what would've happened if she'd stayed downstairs. Riding him on the couch, his hand fisted in her hair, her mouth on his cock. Then she swallowed the piece of him she'd collected, sending all those thoughts, every delirious fantasy, through the magic tethering their spirits.

The spell was like a spider, delivering a dream from one web to another.

CHAPTER SEVEN

T EHLOR NILSEN SLEPT LIKE a baby.

She woke a half-hour after sunrise, body free of aches and stiffness, and stretched beneath her comforter. Incense smoke and leftover cannabis still tainted the air, but her mind was clear and her muscles loose. She turned to look at Gunnhild who stood on the empty left-side pillow, twitching her pink nose.

"Bet he slept like shit," Tehlor whispered.

Gunnhild crept closer and set her tiny paws on Tehlor's jaw.

"You're hungry, huh? All right, I'm up."

Tehlor scooped Gunnhild into her palm and kissed her. She slid out of bed and tiptoed across the room to Gunnhild's space on her waist-high dresser. She refilled the free-standing water bottle and opened the top drawer, digging out a bag of dried edamame, carrots, and seeds. After the rat's bowl was full, she topped the medley with two yogurt chips.

While Gunnhild ate, Tehlor found a half-clean bralette and a pair of yoga shorts. She secured her long, unruly locks with a wide-mouthed clip and tiptoed down the hall, slipping soundlessly into her studio.

She hadn't bought Lincoln a bed-set yet, mostly because she couldn't fathom giving it up. She'd attached a balance bar to the far wall and studied her movements in the sliding closet doors—mirrored from top to bottom—like she had when she was a girl. In there, she was her rawest self. Uncaged and unrefined, deliberately messy despite the assumption of grace most people attached to ballet.

She rested her hand on the balance bar, rose to her tiptoes, and stretched her leg backward, aiming her foot toward the ceiling. She turned her hips out and lowered her torso, bracing her free hand on her shin. The penché pulled nicely, stretching deep in her hamstrings and hip flexors. She closed her eyes. Shifted forward and bounced across the floor, hopping into a split leap.

"You're a dancer," Lincoln said, like someone would say *oh* after solving a riddle. He stood in the doorway, gripping the top of the frame, wearing his human face.

"I was," she said. She eyed him over her shoulder and lifted her right leg, stretching it high. "How'd you sleep?"

He leveled her with a patient but knowing glare. Dark circles purpled his eyes. "You need to recharge."

"I feel great, honestly."

"What're you afraid of?" Lincoln challenged. He dropped his arms and crossed them, leaning casually against the door.

Tehlor dropped into the splits, biting back a wince when her bad knee flexed too far. She pushed the soles of her feet toward the floor. One ankle popped. Pain flared hot in her shin. She watched Lincoln shift his weight from one foot to the other and wondered if he felt her discomfort the same way she caught the frayed edge of his curiosity. The more they picked at each other, the further they stepped into each other's spiritual planes. What a nasty, sticky thing Tehlor probably was, all bone-shard and shoddy magic.

"I'm not afraid," she said, lowering her chest. "I sleep with who I want when I want."

"So, it's a me problem," he said, laughing.

She came out of the stretch and got to her feet, rolling her eyes. "It's an *us* problem."

"Explain."

"I don't do anything without being sure of it."

"That's a lie, Tehlor."

"Fine, I don't do anything unless it serves me."

Lincoln fidgeted with his labradorite necklace. His smile waned. "And what makes you think I wouldn't serve you?"

Her stomach dropped. She quirked an eyebrow, masking a surge of adrenaline with a fake laugh. *Don't*, she thought, chastising herself. *Don't let him see you weak.* She sidestepped him in the doorway, but before she could brush past him, Lincoln grasped her elbow.

"It's foolish to underestimate me," he said, low and rasped.

Tehlor flashed a grin and leaned closer, mouth inches from his chin. "*Uwu,*" she teased, mockingly high-pitched. "*Ara-ara—*"

Lincoln palmed her face and gave a gentle shove. He laughed, boyish and genuine, and she did, too. Laughter came too easily, felt too natural. She cleared her throat and pointed at the stairs.

"We'll try a transference spell. Nothin' extreme," she said, nodding, convincing herself. "You good with that?"

He snorted. "Yeah, I'm good with that."

"Good. Eat something. Can't have you sleepless *and* fatigued."

Tehlor strode down the hall to her bedroom. She expected to hear footsteps on the stairs, but when she looked over her shoulder, Lincoln was still there, watching her walk away.

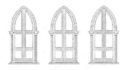

Silver sunlight slipped through the skinny cracks in the blinds, striping the living room windowsill.

Lincoln lit a pillar candle and placed it on the floor beside three others. He'd dressed in a basic long-sleeve and denim and his socked feet made annoying, scuffing sounds on the carpet beneath the coffee table. Tehlor eyed him from the kitchen, stirring cinnamon into a cup of cabernet. He plopped down inside the makeshift chalk circle and offered his hand to Gunnhild. The rat crawled into his palm, and he lifted her up. Tehlor shot Gunnhild a narrow look—*what the fuck are you doing*—but her familiar simply perched on Lincoln's shoulder, cleaned her whiskers, and played at innocence.

"Let's not call any demons today, all right," Tehlor said, dropping a cardamom star into the reddish liquid. "This is a transference spell. Me borrowing from you."

Lincoln rolled his eyes. "Yeah, I know what a transference spell is."

"Well, you're sure good at *taking*, hence the demon, murder, brujería bullshit. Just want to make sure we're on the same page," she teased, and brought the charged wine into the living room, setting it in the center of the circle beside her boline. She went to her knees and sat back on her ankles, flicking her gaze from Gunnhild to Lincoln. She pointed at his necklace. "C'mon, take it off. I need you raw and wolfy, Michael Corvin."

"One more dog joke and I'll drown you in a lake."

"That was a werewolf joke," she corrected, scoffing. Lincoln cocked his head, confused. She furrowed her brow. "Underworld? Kate Beckinsale? The vinyl onesie—*really?*" She gaped when he shook his head. "Are you, like, *gay* gay? Do you even *like* women?"

"I'm whatever the new bisexual is."

"Pansexual and bisexual are a little different—"

"Please, for the love of God, can we do the spell?" He stripped away his necklace. The cloaking spell peeled up and off like ash. All at once, the human mask Lincoln donned shimmered and shook as if a camera had gone in and out of focus, rapidly. She wasn't sure she'd ever get used to it—watching him come apart, come back together.

Tehlor snickered. "Fine, fine. Okay, I'll need that," she said, pointing at his hand.

Lincoln scooted closer and offered his palm.

She inhaled, reaching inward, gathering energy, and brought her boline to his skin. Blood seeped beneath the white-handled blade, flowing from an insignificant wound. A tiny line opened on the heel of her palm, too, following sharp steel against his skin. Carefully, she took his hand and smeared blood across her face. His thumb clipped her mouth, accidentally intimate. She watched his ears twitch, and his pupils expand, and resisted the urge to sink her teeth into his wrist.

Concentration took the utmost importance in any transference spell but being near Lincoln made focusing difficult. *Get it together.* Tehlor tunneled toward the source of his magic, sifting through their shared, sticky threads until she found the place where his energy collided with her own. A small, surprised breath caught in Lincoln's throat. He snatched her bloody hand and squeezed. Suddenly, Tehlor's vision blurred, quivered, changed. She saw her own face, streaked red, eyes clouded white, lips moving around soft spellwork.

She'd stepped into Lincoln's mind, and he'd stepped into hers, and their conjoined magic thrashed and collided.

Let me in.

She flipped her hand over in his and gripped, palm to palm, lifeline to lifeline. He was chaos where it mattered. Wild, debauched, and fucking terrifying. His spirit snapped at her, sharp and metallic, like a sword pulled from cinders. She couldn't shy away from him. Couldn't deflect or shield herself. The entire point of the spell was to absorb a piece of him, but she didn't know how to take what he wouldn't give. Vorðr be damned, Lincoln Stone was not simple, or gentle, or weak.

Tehlor gritted her teeth and grappled for his other hand, finding purchase on his forearm. She rose to her knees and loomed over him, yanking out of his hold to seize his face between her hands.

Command him. But she knew better.

"Blessed by Fenrir, keeper of old, I ask for assistance," she hissed, inhaling the breath he exhaled. "Give unto me that which you do not need, guardian of Valhalla." Her tongue almost tripped, but she forced the words out. "How I beg of thee."

Lincoln made a growlish noise, like laughter but worse. He gripped her hipbones, held on, and all at once, like a circuit blowing, his power surged through her. She saw her jaw slacken, watched her eyes close, and made a point to thrust her soul toward him, to be present and attentive, to hook her thorny spirit around the ichor he poured into her. She came back to herself the same way a person woke from fainting, except quicker. The fuzzy edges of reality cracked into place. Her heart hammered, drumming in her ears, elbows, stomach. She felt sick for a moment, but the nausea passed as soon as the room stopped spinning.

Well, fuck. Not your grandma's transference spell, I guess.

Tehlor recognized vitality. It soaked her bones—raw, unkempt power—and like a dying hearth stoked with fresh flint, her magic flared red hot.

Lincoln breathed heavily. His wide chest rose and fell, and he lowered his ears. His attentive, gentle expression betrayed how tightly he held himself.

"Where'd you get all that," she sputtered. Giddy laughter jumped up and out of her.

"Hell," he purred.

She sank back on her heels. Her hands slipped from his face and dropped into her lap. He let her go, but his fingertips scraped the place where the top of her pencil pants met her sweater, brushing a strip of exposed skin. The air was charged with what they'd done. Energy crackled and popped. Gunnhild must've skittered off Lincoln's shoulder, because she stood on her haunches outside the circle, watching from underneath the coffee table.

Tehlor grinned, catching her breath. "See, being my Vorðr isn't so bad, huh?"

He hummed and tilted his head, assessing her with a slow, mindful pass. "You carry a lot, you know. It's why your power doesn't stick. Your bones are slippery with guilt." His tongue clicked on the last word, striking her like a rubber band. "You're ashamed of useless—"

"Watch your mouth," she snapped.

"Lions don't apologize to gazelle. Bears don't cry over dead deer."

"Okay, wise man, well—"

"You're a Viking witch who held council with the goddess of death," he said, bewildered. His thumb clipped her chin, squeezing gently. When he leaned closer, she thought for a brief, bright moment that he might kiss her, but he just smiled, sending laughter coasting across her mouth. "And you feel bad because you refuse to entertain mediocrity?"

"Refusing to *entertain mediocrity* and hurting people on purpose isn't the same," she said.

"If you don't stop punishing yourself for being ambitious, you won't get shit when it comes to magic, or power, *or* control."

"So, you don't feel bad for what you did to Bishop?" She leaned away from him, dislodging his hand from her chin. "Not even a little bit?"

Lincoln's throat flexed. He tightened his jaw. His two-toned eyes went cold, his unrelenting gaze set on her. *Mistake*, instinct said, blaring inside her like a siren, *oops, uh oh, bad call, abort*. He chewed the inside of his cheek and brought his hands to his lap, letting her go. The set of his shoulders made him appear bigger, somehow. She expected him to snap at her, at least. Seize her by the throat again, maybe. But he simply shook his head.

"Mourning the life you built with someone and feeling bad for how it ended are two different things, Tehlor. I don't have any regrets if that's what you're asking."

"Neither do I," she said. *Fucking insulting*.

"Yeah, you do." He placed two fingers on her sternum and gave a gentle push.

She lost her balance and plopped on her rear. "*I don't!*"

"Then what's holding you back, huh? Because I was just inside your head. I know you're ashamed of—"

"I'm allowed to grieve the woman I could've been while honoring who I am, Lincoln," she snapped. She braced herself on the floor with her palms and screwed her mouth into a snarl. She thought of dancing. Pictured the wedding she'd never have, the children she'd never rear, the notoriety she'd pissed away. "Just like you're allowed to mourn your cozy little life with Bishop while you chase the promise of power with me. Grief and ambition can coexist."

"Yeah, and what're you grieving? Fake friends from high school? A pink leotard? Some guy who *called the corners* with you one time? C'mon, be for real."

Tehlor scraped her teeth over her bottom lip. Gunnhild crept closer, standing on her haunches to press her front paws to Tehlor's forearm. *Asshole.* His power smoldered in her core, emboldening the familiar runic magic buzzing in the ink on her knuckles and the tattoo on her throat. *Freya, grant me grace*, she silently chanted, staring hard at the man across from her.

Lincoln didn't know her past, and he certainly couldn't tell the future.

Keep underestimating me, she thought, sighing through her nose. *Keep testing me, sorcerer.*

"I work today. Can you do some research on Haven and the Breath of Judas while I'm gone? We need to know what we're up against," she said.

Lincoln blinked. He parted his lips to speak, then pulled his mouth shut and cinched his brow confusedly.

Tehlor stood and picked up Gunnhild, placing the rat on her shoulder.

"That's it, then?" he asked, snorting defiantly.

"Cool, thanks," she said, ignoring his question, and strode toward the staircase.

With their power mingling—thrashing and chewing inside her—Tehlor Nilsen was on the verge of transcendence, explosiveness, or susceptibility, and she didn't have the space necessary to deal with any of it. Not when she was transcending into someone who *wanted* Lincoln, in every dangerous and disastrous way, and not when she was in the finite place before exploding, creating wreckage where there was the possibility for safety, and not when she was unmoored, susceptible to his prying, vulnerable and torn open, and dying to be held.

Tehlor and Lincoln didn't speak for three days.

She'd imagined plunging a screwdriver through the top of his hand to get his attention. She'd thought about crawling into his lap, too. But mostly, she'd cursed the claustrophobic townhouse for its petite frame and forged stoicism whenever they'd bumped each other in the kitchen, caught each other in the hall, or strode past each other in the living room. They had mere days before the cookout, and after that, only hours to prepare for the revival. She didn't have time for petty games, and she didn't have the patience to responsibly handle the silent treatment, either.

It was all disgustingly childish—feigning avoidance; the *theater* of it all. Still, she retreated to the spare bedroom, dressed in sweatpants and a cropped sweatshirt, and bundled her hair into a ponytail. Moonstrike clung to her, turned soil and freshly printed books, fickle energy and incense smoke, and her calves ached from standing on her tiptoes, arranging amethyst cathedrals on a tall shelf. She blew out a sigh and bent into a plié.

"There's no concrete evidence of the Breath of Judas existing," Lincoln said. His voice cut through the quiet, drawing her attention like an arrow. He stood in the doorway. Wolfish ears twitched atop his head. "And no clear-cut ritual or how-to. If Haven has the relic, and I believe they do, then they're just as much in the dark about it as we are."

"I doubt that," Tehlor said.

It was the first conversation they'd had since the transference spell. All business; no fluff.

"The Breath of Judas has a paper trail. San Crisogono, then Notre Dame. The Vatican, even. Sure, there's no *official* documentation of its power, but rumors come to life somehow. All myth starts as word-of-mouth." She stretched toward the floor and grabbed her ankles, turning to rest her cheek on her thigh, looking at him. "What makes you think Haven has it?"

"A division in the hierarchy of the clergy last year. One side wanted the church to run like a business, the other wanted a militia."

"And the militia came to Gideon," Tehlor said, defeated.

"Seems that way, yeah."

"What do you believe the relic does?"

Lincoln considered her carefully. He stepped into the room and moved in front of her, blocking her view of the mirror.

"I think it's exactly what we originally believed; a necromantic tool used to control corpses. There's more to it, I'm sure. I doubt accessing purgatory through the living essence of Christ's betrayer is a walk in the park, but." He shrugged.

Tehlor straightened and cracked her neck. She sidestepped him and resumed her gentle stretches, keeping her gaze cemented on her reflection. She hadn't considered what communication might be like with someone she respected, wanted, and feared because she'd never stayed in a relationship long enough to find all three in a person. She'd always been the one doing the leaving. The heartbreaker. The bad thing that happened to good people.

Lincoln Stone was a consequence—karma coming back to sink its teeth into her—and Tehlor hated how her heart bent toward him.

"What'd you do?" He slid closer, stepping in front of her again. "Break someone's little heart? Steal something valuable?"

She took the opportunity to use him for balance and set her hand on his shoulder, flexing her knees.

"Both, yeah," she said.

"And?"

She swallowed hard, grinding her back teeth. There was always something. A truly terrible deed executed clumsily enough to leave a scar, but *no one* liked talking about that shit, and she'd made a point to stay silent on the subject of her teenage-Tonya-Harding incident with everyone except her fucking lawyer.

Lincoln placed his hand on her waist when she stood upright. His thumb followed the top of her sweatpants, gingerly brushing fair skin. "C'mon, my ex cut my heart in half and put my body in a wall. Can't be that bad."

"I shattered a girl's kneecap after she got the lead in Swan Lake," Tehlor said. She offered a small, forced smile, and lifted both brows, saddling him with an expectant look. "A scout from NYU offered her a scholarship after the performance and I…" She huffed out a laugh. "…lost my shit. I was sixteen, busting my ass in advanced classes, on track to graduate early and spread so fuckin' thin I couldn't think, couldn't cope, couldn't rationalize. I swung a thirty-pound dumbbell into the side of her leg at the gym two days later. Smashed her patella into pieces."

"Ouch."

"It was over for me after that. GPA? Shot. College applications? Useless. Got out of juvi when I was eighteen, packed my shit, and used my college fund to buy this place." She gestured around the studio with a flick of her wrist. "I could've gone to Julliard. Could've moved to Paris, could've met someone nice, settled down, and opened my own studio. But I got *mad* instead." She hung her head and grinned cruelly at the ceiling. "I was a foolish little girl," she whispered, harsh and pained. "Powerless and petty and too pissed to function."

"That doesn't make you a foolish woman," he said, steadying her as she arced backward, stretching her spine.

"I *am* a foolish woman." *You make me foolish.*

Lincoln ran his hand from her waist to her nape, dusting his fingers along her spine. He gripped the back of her neck and held her steady as she straightened.

"That foolish little girl evolved into the witch you are today. Convening with gods, harnessing power, raising the dead." He met her eyes and reached into his pocket, retrieving his labradorite necklace. He slipped the cord over his head. His human form manifested like lightning, sudden and surreal. "The thought of you rotting away in a French chateau, married to a loan officer, puttering around the kitchen, fixing dinner, setting the table..." He laughed in his throat and leaned closer, pressing a raspy whisper to the corner of her mouth. "Disgusts me."

She narrowed her eyes. Everything beneath her navel squeezed. "I imagined you didn't think of me much at all."

"Can't lie to me, witchling." He stroked the side of her throat with his thumb. "I'm part of you now, remember?"

Tehlor warmed against him. Her heart thundered, and her face flared hot. She wanted to know if he could feel her lightheadedness, taste the desire sparking in her mouth, or track the quickness of her blood.

He hummed. "So, that's your big, nasty secret, huh? Wanting something so badly it drove you to violence?"

"You don't seem impressed."

"I'm not," he assured and tilted his head.

She tasted his breath. Coffee. Brown sugar creamer. *I hate this.* Hated waiting. Hated how easily he'd detonated her. Hated how three days of calculated silence had led to this. But she didn't hate him, and he didn't hate her, and that was a lovely, frightening surprise.

Tehlor craned toward him. "C'mon, sorcerer. Don't be a fucking coward."

Lincoln kissed her. It was the kind of kiss she'd only experienced twice before. Once when she was drunk and lonely, searching for a spark of connection on a crowded dancefloor, and again with the girl she'd battered, the rival who'd stolen her spotlight and shattered her heart. She met him with vigor and hunger, searching for sustenance between his parted lips. Maybe she was a challenge to him, something to conquer, or maybe she was a collector's item, something to poach. Either way, Tehlor Nilsen was wild because of him, graceless and *wanting.*

Guilt panged, shaped like Bishop's name, but Tehlor didn't stop when Lincoln backed her against the wall. Her tailbone smacked the balance bar and she grabbed onto it, anchoring herself as he pried lovingly at her mouth, kissing her deeply, thoroughly, with fevered patience she hadn't expected. He made a soft noise, like a moan but raspier, at the snag of her teeth on his lip, and pressed his hips between her thighs, forcing her legs apart.

Lincoln cracked his eyes open. "You brought me back to make you more powerful, right?"

Tehlor sighed, resisting the urge to grind into his pelvis. "At first, yeah."

"What about now?"

"Can we talk about this later—"

"Tehlor."

She gripped the balance bar harder and snaked her free hand from his shoulder to his nape, clutching him the same way he'd held her moments ago.

"Fine. Yes, Lincoln. I pulled you out of the wall and sewed the dog head between your shoulders because I wanted to be more powerful. I'm sorry, I know, bad move. How many times do you want me to say it?"

"I read about being a vorðr," he said, sliding his hand beneath the waistband of her sweatpants. He palmed her hip, teasing at the soft pout of her ass. "It means guardian, I think. Protector."

"Sometimes, yeah," she said, breathless. "Guard, guardian—whatever. Same thing."

Lincoln's mouth ticked upward. He kissed her again, quick and full, then pressed his lips to her jaw, lower, suckling sweetly on her pulse. "You're always in a hurry, you know that? Lookin' for a shortcut, tryin' to bypass shit wherever you can." His teeth grazed the smooth curve where her shoulder met her throat. "I can make you powerful, but you need to let that guilt go." He dragged his hand out of her sweatpants and splayed it across her stomach, feeling upward across her sternum, fingertips featherlight between her breasts. "I can teach you patience; I can give you power." Laughter gusted across her neck, gritty and tempered. "I can make you worse," he whispered, pressing his clothed cock between her legs, "if you let me."

Tehlor grasped his face with both hands and brought his mouth to her own. *I can make you worse.* His voice reverberated, bouncing off bone, rippling across muscle.

For years, she'd made spiritual sacrifices, hunted relentlessly for access to godhood, sliced magic out of her skin, and stolen what she failed to excavate from within. And for years, she'd stewed in pathetic self-inflicted solitude, revering the power she craved while punishing the past life she didn't have the strength to bury.

"Do it," she said, sighing each word like a prayer. "Go ahead and try."

CHAPTER EIGHT

T HE PRE-COOKED, PERFECTLY SEASONED scalloped potatoes slid neatly into a casserole dish alongside garlic green beans. Tehlor sprinkled a bit of parmesan on top of the food and swatted her palms together, shaking away crumbs. She looked over her cookout contribution and sighed.

Lincoln bounced down the staircase dressed in an army-green turtleneck and dark denim. His labradorite pendant was concealed beneath the chic cable-knit material, and his two-toned eyes flicked from the not-quite casserole on the countertop to Tehlor's face.

He snickered. "Store bought?"

"Restaurant take-out, obviously."

She met his steady gaze and remembered two days ago, her fingers knotted in his short hair, holding his face between her legs, then her back pressed against the wall, watching his shoulders flex in the mirror across the room, her feet bouncing, his hips snapping. Sex was different with him—unlike anything she'd experienced before. She'd felt every shred of the act. Him, widening her. How she felt, warm and tight, squeezing him. She'd endured the growing heat of his climax while coming down from her own, gasping and clinging to him. His sharp, explosive pleasure had weighed heavy on her oversensitive body, blurring her vision, causing her head to spin. It was a new bond, spirits and bodies, magic and flesh. Too intense to name, maybe.

Being with Lincoln, seeing herself through his eyes, feeling her body through his own, brought the surreal, primal truth of their interconnectedness to light.

Tehlor Nilsen would never find another lover like *that*. She could never make someone else her vorðr. The thought paralyzed her.

She imagined herself an insect accidentally perched on a carnivorous plant. Stuck; petals folding in. But Lincoln had been a conscious choice, and Tehlor was not defenseless. She found her feet glued, regardless. Limbs frozen, struggling against the inevitable.

"Nice dress," he said.

She shimmied her arms, shaking out the long bell sleeves on her fanciful garment, decorated like blue and white Qinghua pottery. Small buttons were centered neatly on her throat and her wrists looked oddly petite shackled by satin cuffs. She'd roped the top of her hair into a French braid and the rest fell past her shoulders in tousled waves. The gold bands stacked on her fingers matched the thrifted crucifix strung around her neck. She felt like a beautiful fraud. Like Mary Magdalene, a reformed whore.

"Bet it belonged to someone's grandma," she said, sealing tinfoil over the dish. "Heels or flats?"

"Modest heels."

"Yeah, I don't own any of those, Clifford. What's the point of cramming your feet into a pair of heels if they're not *high?*"

Lincoln silently repeated the name, mouthing *Clifford* confusedly.

"Fine. Yes, heels. But wear the cardigan, too," he said.

Tehlor deflated, saddling him with a pitiful frown. "Seriously? The atrocity you found on the two-dollar rack?"

Laughter rumbled in his throat. "Yeah, that one. C'mon. Coat, rat, keys. We shouldn't be late."

She seethed at him as she rounded the breakfast bar. His hand ghosted her waist, just barely. She remembered kissing the side of his bony muzzle during a shared shower and tracing the autopsy scars carved into his torso.

People rarely imprinted on her. Rarely left a mark. Again, she thought of a Venus fly trap.

Her keen eyes snapped to his own, searching for any indication that she'd infiltrated his thoughts the same way he'd apprehended hers. Lincoln, like always, seemed steady and unchanged. *Asshole.* She shrugged on the depressing white cardigan, then followed it with a long wool jacket. When she clucked her tongue, Gunnhild scampered from her enclosure and crawled into Tehlor's palm. She lowered her familiar into a leather purse and slung the bag over her shoulder. At last, she slid on a pair of beige heels and stuck her foot out at Lincoln, lifting a brow.

"See? They're not hoochie," she said, turning her ankle back and forth.

"Showing too much calf is *hoochie* to these people, sweetheart." He grabbed the casserole and nodded toward the hallway. "Go on."

Wind blew loose snow from fenceposts and rooves, and the chilly night nipped at exposed skin. Tehlor hurried to the truck and slid inside, shivering. She set her purse in the middle seat and revved the engine, glancing at herself in the rearview mirror. Mascara, rosy blush, lip balm, dollish and toned-down. She scrunched her nose. Lincoln watched the road while she drove, one hand resting on her purse, granting Gunnhild a finger to place her paws on.

"Don't mention the relic," he said. "Don't hint at it, don't look for it, don't give them any reason to suspect that's what we're after."

"The sweet one—Andy, *Amy*—already confirmed they'll be pulling out all the stops at the revival; we need to know what that means." Tehlor drummed her thumbs on the steering wheel, slowing down as they approached the cookie-cutter neighborhood where the gathering was taking place.

"Then let it be organic. Ask about the schedule, what you can help with—all the innocent shit. I'll try to get close to Paul."

"Phillip," Tehlor corrected.

"Whatever. At this point, I highly doubt he's pulling the strings, but I'll still feel him out."

"I thought you were *sure* he's the ringleader. If not him, who?"

"His wife participated in several publicized interviews after Haven split." Lincoln slid a pointed stare in her direction. "Which means she's the mouthpiece. In situations like this, the person addressing the media is usually the one in control. That's all you. Don't fuck it up."

"Oh, c'mon, blondie's harmless," Tehlor said, snorting.

She parked along the sidewalk two houses down and turned off the headlights, idling in the heated truck-cab.

He shook his head. "I doubt that. She's too cautious about us. Clearly, there's something at stake for her."

"Or she's just a bitch."

"You're a bitch. She's something else."

Tehlor shrugged. He wasn't wrong. "Fine. You good? We good?"

"We're good, let's go."

"Stay in there," Tehlor mumbled, fastening her purse closed with Gunnhild safely inside.

The two-story house was pretty and white, blanketed in snow and topped with a smoking chimney. Frosty blue shutters stood out against the clean exterior, Adirondack chairs decorated the porch, and shadows darkened gilded windows, flickering like ghosts beyond the glass. Lincoln took Tehlor's palm, lacing their fingers, and raised his free hand to knock politely at the door.

An immediate hush came over the chatter inside as if a fox had breached the entrance of a busy chicken coop.

Weird. Goosebumps scaled Tehlor's arms. She inhaled deeply and glanced at Lincoln, but before she could whisper *what the fuck was that* the door swung open.

Phillip flashed a princely grin. "Friends, welcome."

Lincoln extended his hand and clasped Philip's palm. "Thank you for opening your home to us."

"This is Daniel's rental, actually," the pastor said, gesturing inside with a sweep of his arm. "Rose and I are grateful to have a supportive congregation. What we've built at Haven really transcends the typical couch-to-pew routine, you know? It's a lifestyle for us, and it's all for him." He pointed at the ceiling with his index finger and pressed his mouth into a thin, pensive smile. He repeated the last three words, "All for him," nodding.

Tehlor forced a smile and nodded along. *Fuckin' psychopath.*

"I'll take this to the kitchen," she said, like a good little housewife, and lifted the casserole dish.

Lincoln met her eyes and smiled, granting her a curt nod. "Good idea, honey."

As unnatural as it was, she channeled meekness and lowered her eyes, smiling at the floor. "Good to see you, Pastor Phillip."

"Same to you, Tehlor. I'm sure the girls are in the kitchen. Fix yourself some wine," Phillip said. He touched her elbow, like a teacher, like someone used to touching whomever he pleased, however he pleased, and then swatted Lincoln on the back, steering him toward the living room. "Lincoln, how do you take your whiskey?"

The stark entryway led to a wide, bland hall. She scanned the eggshell walls and paused at the mouth of the staircase on the left, listening to footsteps creak on the second story. She turned, stepping into the kitchen. Her heels clicked the tile and she remembered to smile at Rose and Amy, surrounded by chittering church ladies.

Amy whipped toward Tehlor and gasped through a grin, bouncing excitedly. Rose gave Tehlor a cold once over. Her disapproving gaze lingered on Tehlor's tall shoes for a heartbeat too long before she took a sip from a sleek, stemless wine glass and resumed whatever conversation she'd paused.

The women in the kitchen embodied a chic, clean-girl aesthetic. Slick ponytails, minimalist makeup, savannah cotton blouses, dainty Christian jewelry—crucifixes, rose gold bands, and stone-carved rosaries. Trendy, taupe flats. Designer athleisure. Bodies meant for missionary position, green juices, and gestation.

Tehlor pitied them. She did, seriously—Girl Scout's honor. But she hated them more.

"You made it," Amy cooed, coming around the marble island to take the casserole dish. She set it down and peeled off the foil, making a pleased noise. "Wow, you're quite the cook, babe! Is this a family recipe?"

"Lincoln's mom," she lied, smiling wide for a chorus of *aww* and *how sweet*.

"Well, thank you for blessing us with her tradition. Can I get you some wine? Kombucha? I think Candice brought an apricot mocktail, too," Amy said.

"Wine, please."

"Red or white?" Rose interjected. She met Tehlor's gaze and lifted her chin, offering a delicate smile. Her cashmere sweater drooped over one shoulder, stark atop a soft, sandy dress with skinny straps.

Somehow, the question felt like a test. Tehlor considered, tongue pressed hard against the roof of her mouth, before she shrugged and said, "Whatever you're having."

Cabernet ribboned from a dark bottle and splashed at the bottom of a spotless glass. Rose made a point to set the beverage in front of Tehlor rather than handing it to her. The women in the kitchen postured, lions in a pride, following Rose's example. Tehlor had been introduced abruptly, carelessly, and the only way forward was to roll onto her back and show her underbelly to the matriarch. She bowed her head and took the glass, sipping gingerly.

"I love your tattoos, Tehlor," one of the women said. Her fiery hair was smoothed into a low, modest braid, and her teeth looked expensive. She gestured to her own neck, swallowing nervously. "Is that a bird or...?"

"It's a Nordic hawk." Tehlor traded her glass from one hand to the other.

Quiet snaked through the house. Somewhere in a nearby room, men laughed. Something moved upstairs and Tehlor blinked, shielding a sudden bolt of fear. *Not a single kid*, she thought. *I've seen no children.* The realization shouldn't have made her afraid, but it did. It terrified her. She snapped back to the conversation and held out her hand, displaying her inked knuckles.

Bless these lies for the truth takes root, deadly and full of thorns. "Norse runes, too. My ancestors heard the Lord's good word, but the transition was painful." *We were eradicated. Slaughtered. Forced.* "So, I got these as a reminder that anything is possible. If Christ could reach their hearts, he can certainly have mine." Bile scorched her throat. *Forgive me, Freya. Fill me with gratitude, Odin Allfather.* "They're a bit crude, I know."

Another wife tilted her head as if she agreed. "Remember when Ashleigh got her serpent tattoo after the divorce? Such a shame."

"Ashleigh went on her way, Meredith. The Lord will keep her," Rose said.

In unison, every woman in the kitchen said, "The Lord will keep her," except for Tehlor.

Every mental alarm that could've rang out did so at the very same time. Jaws music. The theme song from Halloween. Admiral Ackbar hollering *it's a trap!* Fire alarms, air-raid sirens, and the iconic slasher movie *ching ching ching*. She'd understood Haven was a whacky fucking cult before walking into the cookout, but she hadn't realized how disquieting being a part of the charade would be until right then, standing in a kitchen, listening to Haven housewives echo each other in prayer.

Tehlor cleared her throat and repeated the phrase. "The Lord will keep her."

"Ashleigh used to be a member at Haven," Amy explained, cringing. "We tried to come to an understanding, but going against Phillip's decision to keep the—"

"God forgives all. As his shepherds, we must protect the flock," Rose interrupted. She shot Amy a silencing glare before switching her attention to Tehlor. "She posed a threat to our mission, so we parted ways. Amicably, of course."

"Of course," Tehlor said. She wondered if Ashleigh was alive. If she'd been sacrificed on a stone table or left to rot in a confessional. She sipped her wine and cleared the chalky bite from her throat. "Is everyone excited for the revival?"

"Oh yes," someone said.

"Very much so."

"Obviously, babe!"

"Tehlor, you're looking forward to being baptized, aren't you?" Rose asked, careening over delighted voices. Every sound was snuffed out. She lifted her brows and tipped her head, snaring Tehlor in another challenging stare. "Under the moonlight, surrounded by those who will bring you closer to God. You're one of a few scheduled baptisms, actually. Kimberly, of course, the new carrier, and then Mary, Lucas's new betrothed."

Carrier. Tehlor cocked her head.

"Daniel, too," Amy added.

Rose nodded. Her smile came and went, as fleeting as a hummingbird. "Yes, Daniel will be anointed and returned to his wife, sinless and reborn."

"Wife?" Tehlor asked.

Amy smiled, weak and solemn. "Yeah, we've been married for a little over a year now."

"And he isn't baptized?"

"Baptism isn't a one-time blessing at Haven. We baptize our brothers and sisters after transgressions, honoring both the sin and the act of washing it away. Baptism is a reintroduction to God and his people, so we invite newcomers and anyone in the congregation to participate. You claim your sin, drown it, and then resurface as God intended. New, clean," Rose said, drawing out the second word. "A disciple remade."

So, Rose and Phillip controlled the home Amy and Daniel rented in Gideon. It wasn't *un*predictable, but the calculated manipulation still made Tehlor reconsider the ease of her and Lincoln's little heist. Haven felt dangerous the same way most large-scale organizations did—oppressive and volatile—but it was something else, too. Radical. Like a starving thing let in from the cold, looking for food, hunting for resources. Tehlor remembered to smile and offered an appreciative nod. She sipped her wine, turned toward another glistening Haven girl, and sighed blissfully.

"I can't wait to see what midnight mass has in store," Tehlor said.

The women exchanged glances, bright-eyed and secretive.

Rose whispered, "Great things," so seriously Tehlor's breath caught. *Maybe Lincoln's right. Maybe Rose is the ringleader.* "Obedience is holy. In Haven we trust."

Again, the kitchen filled with radiant voices. "Obedience is holy. In Haven we trust."

Tehlor swallowed the rest of her wine. "Amen."

Laughter boomed in the hall followed by footsteps. All at once, the women scattered, grabbing plates and serving spoons. Nervousness lit in Tehlor's stomach. She didn't know whether to mimic their behavior or wait for instructions. Everyone moved precisely, still smiling, still chatting, wiping hands, serving each other, saying *thank you*. Once the casserole dishes were properly gutted and the rest of the congregation filtered into the kitchen, Tehlor understood.

Each woman carefully handed a perfectly fixed plate to someone else. A man, specifically. Rose to Phillip, Amy to whom Tehlor assumed to be Daniel. An undercurrent of *thank you sweetheart* and *appreciate you, honey* hummed like a beehive.

Lincoln appeared at her side before she realized he'd entered the room. He placed his hand on her lower back, palm secure on her tailbone. It was a risky gesture, touching her intentionally, intimately. She hadn't seen other couples show affection. Handholding, yes. Some mild embraces, sure. But partners didn't tug at each other like Lincoln tugged at her, hauling her close to his side. He wrapped his hand around her hip and splayed his fingers over the soft pout below her navel, scratching playfully.

"Have you eaten already?" Lincoln asked. "I can fix you somethin'."

The question burned through the room. She glanced around, unsure if she should jump into her role as a good-to-do-wife or let the attention fester.

"Oh, Lincoln, I can get you a plate, dear," Amy said, batting at the air. "Here, let me—"

"That's all right, Amy. I can get it," he said, cutting her off.

Amy paused mid-reach. Her hand hovered over the stacked plates before she brought it to her chest, clutching her wrist awkwardly.

Lincoln stepped around Tehlor, grabbed a plate, and went to work assembling food. "Mac 'n cheese, babe?"

Tehlor nodded. "Sure."

The silence ballooned. Tehlor kept her chin lifted, smiling first at Amy, then at Rose.

"We take pride in serving our husbands," Rose said, lightly, as if it was a perfectly normal thing to say. She rubbed Pastor Phillip's back. *Awkward*, Tehlor thought. "It must be a treat to be doted on, Tehlor."

Tehlor opened her mouth to speak, but Lincoln was too quick.

"Husbands, love your wives as Christ so loved the church," he said, pinning Rose with a thoughtful stare. "Ephesians, right?"

Rose inhaled sharply. "I believe so."

"Let each of you love his wife as himself." Lincoln handed Tehlor a plate, two-toned eyes skimming her face. "We're equal in everything except creation. In our relationship, only she can do that," he tapped her chin with his thumb and winked. "But don't worry, Rose, she dotes on me, too."

The tension remained. Women glanced at their men while their men looked at Phillip, waiting for confrontation, acceptance, or a subject change. Tehlor forked a green bean into her mouth and stayed close to Lincoln. She met Amy's eyes on a flighty pass and tried to send a mental signal, to channel calm and security. But Amy immediately looked at the ground and Tehlor thought for sure they'd blown their cover.

"To Lincoln and Tehlor," Pastor Phillip said, lifting his whiskey glass. "New to our flock, but already channeling Christ-like behavior. Guys, take notes. Protect, provide, and spread the good word. That's our duty."

Tehlor exhaled, relieved. She beamed at Phillip and Rose. "We're blessed to be here."

Lincoln lifted his glass. "To Haven," he said.

The room repeated, "To Haven."

Risk assessment, complete.

Tehlor wanted to look at Lincoln, but she knew better than to meet his eyes. If she looked at him, the congregation might sense her relief. Might catch onto the diabolical magic sparking between them. She ate gingerly. Smiled and nodded at passing conversation. Someone talked about flower arrangements for a wedding. Another person chatted about a new car. She took the chance to glance at pockets and wrists, ankles and hands, assessing each person for weapons, charms, and scars. *Who is capable?* Daniel's knuckles were chewed up. He'd fought before, punched walls or people. *Who is carrying?* Thankfully, she didn't see a holster or dented waistbands, but given Haven's origin and the reason for the internal split, she assumed they were armed.

"Here, honey, let me take this." Amy appeared like a wraith and snuck her slender hand beneath the strap on Tehlor's purse.

Tehlor jolted, slapping her free hand over the bag. "No, it's okay. I've got it."

"Oh, it's fine," she assured, nodding toward a short, wooden cabinet against the wall next to the open doorway, crowned with a pile of mini-backpacks and neutral purses. "I'll put it with the others."

Lincoln patted her hip. "Go ahead."

Don't move, she internally chanted, thinking of the rat hidden in her bag. *Don't you dare move.*

Amy placed Tehlor's purse on the table and swatted her hands together, striding back to Tehlor's side.

"Lincoln, did you get a chance to connect with Daniel? I'm sure you two would get along," Amy said.

Lincoln nodded. "I did. It's good to meet someone else who served."

"Oh, he's army?" Tehlor asked.

Amy's smile tightened. "Marines. He was honorably discharged a few months after we met." She gestured to the sliding glass door that led to the snowy backyard. "I brought s'more supplies, by the way. Figured somethin' sweet might be nice after dinner." Her attention switched to Daniel, standing next to Phillip and Rose. "Dan, can you get the fire going?"

Intentional subject change. Tehlor snuck a glance at Lincoln. He inclined his head, acknowledging her silent note.

Daniel—tall, broad, and swathed in plaid and denim—finished his drink and made for the backdoor. Amy's and Daniel's obvious differences from the rest of Haven didn't go unnoticed. Tehlor hadn't seen it at first, but the closer she looked, the more she understood. Amy, who followed Rose like a puppy, wore a cheap, off-brand jumpsuit and knock-off Birkenstocks. Unlike the expensive attire and spotless Timberland hikers the rest of the men wore, Daniel dressed in Walmart jeans and old military boots.

It shouldn't have been a surprise, but Rose's strategic puppeteering and privileged control over her *bestie* filled Tehlor with rage. She might've been a thief. She certainly knew how to manipulate a situation, hotwire an old car, and knock someone out with an herb combo.

But Tehlor didn't steal from the poor. Her moral compass worked that much, at least.

"Good idea, Mrs. De'voreaux," Phillip said, loudly enough to prompt the rest of the group to finish their meals and step outside.

Eat, Tehlor thought, glancing between Rose, Amy, Candice, Meredith, and whomever the rest of them were. But the women hardly touched their food. Barely nibbled a corncob or munched an orange slice. She thought of dancing. How sustenance had been an exercise in self-control. She spooned more macaroni into her mouth and chewed, forcing herself to imagine a great feast, pitchers of ale, roasted meat surrounded by vegetables—Valhalla.

What a thing, Tehlor thought, remembering the weight of a dumbbell in her hand, how it'd lightened as she swung it, *to love a God to the point of starvation*.

"Can I steal your wifey, Lincoln?" Amy asked, snapping Tehlor back into the present.

Lincoln smirked. He leaned down, pecking Tehlor on the lips. Her marrow burned. "Sure. See you around, *wifey*."

Tehlor hummed, swiping her tongue across her bottom lip, chasing the whiskey on his mouth. "Yeah, all right, hubby. See you in a bit."

"Aren't you two ah-dorable," Amy whined. She took Tehlor by the elbow and guided her down the hall to the coatrack adjacent to the front door. Once they were out of sight, Amy's expression relaxed, falling into a mock cringe. "Sometimes it gets a little stuffy. Not, like, *bad*, you know, but kind of suffocating," she confessed, shoving her arms through a puffy coat. She waited for Tehlor to button her wool jacket before she grabbed her elbow again, steering her toward the door. "I'm glad you're here, though. So glad."

Something heavy hit the floor on the second story, booming through the ceiling. It wasn't loud, but it stole her attention. Like a bowling ball, or a sack of soil, or a body. Tehlor glanced over her shoulder and stumbled onto the porch, pulled by Amy.

"Did you hear that?" Tehlor asked.

"Oh, yeah. It's just my sister," she said, dismissively. She batted at the air and reached past Tehlor, grasping the handle. "She's resting upstairs. Not a big party person, you know?"

"Yeah…" She watched the hallway disappear, cut away by the door swinging shut. *Who the hell are you hiding?* "Me neither, honestly."

Chapter Nine

T EHLOR FOLDED HER ARMS across her chest, shielding herself from a chilly snap of wind. She felt aggressively naked without Gunnhild, like, ridiculously, alarmingly *nude*. She didn't go anywhere without that damn rat. Whether she was shopping at the grocery store, fingering through clothes at a boutique, or sipping a cocktail at a dive bar, Gunnhild was always there, perched on her shoulder, snuggled in her pocket, or tucked carefully inside a purse.

Eight years ago, when Tehlor had bound her spirit to Gunnhild's, offering a year of her predetermined life to Vör, goddess of wisdom, in exchange for an eternal companion, she hadn't realized just how important that little rodent would become. But Gunnhild wasn't just a sacrificial tool or a rare pet-store find. They belonged to each other entirely. When Tehlor died, Gunnhild died, too. Soul for soul. Magic for magic. Being separated from her chipped away at Tehlor's finely crafted church-lady persona, leaving her fidgety and nervous.

Don't do anything stupid, she thought, mentally beaming the command to her familiar.

Amy sighed. Her breath plumed in the air. She relaxed, tilting her head from side to side.

"We can go through the side door," Amy said, gesturing loosely toward the fence around the back half of the property. She tipped her pretty face toward the moon, partially hidden by a cloudy night sky. "Do you ever think God gives us the chance to change our past?"

Tehlor's attention sharpened. "Our God is a forgiving God, isn't he?"

"New Testament, yeah. Old Testament? Not so much." Amy slid a sleek, black vape out of her pocket. Her smile thinned. "Don't tell, okay? Rose doesn't like us to vices."

"Your secret's safe with me."

"I don't know, I just... I think this expansion is such a blessing, you know? We're bringing in new members, hosting a revival, spreading the message..."

"But," Tehlor prompted.

Amy sucked her vape and blew candy-scented vapor at her feet. "But I'm scared," she confessed, bewildered. She furrowed her brow and laughed under her breath, and it was the first time Tehlor recognized her as *real*. "It's stupid, right? To be afraid of what comes after this?"

"It's human," she said, shrugging. "Put your faith in Rose and Phillip. The Lord speaks through them."

"I know," she said, harsh and low, then again, sweeter, "I know."

Ah, Tehlor quietly pondered, taking in Amy De'voreaux, Haven misfit, *you're the lost little lamb, aren't you?*

"It was nice to meet your husband. Plannin' to grow the family anytime soon?" Tehlor tested.

Amy stiffened, but her smile didn't falter. "Children require intent," she said, sucking on her vape again. "I don't know if I'll be the mother Haven needs, but I'd like kids, I think. Motherhood is...

It's daunting. I mean, with Ashleigh..." She paused, granting Tehlor a careful, cautious look.

"I won't say anything," she assured, showing her palms in mock-surrender. "What happened?"

"Nothing *happened*." Amy heaved a sigh, shifting her boot back and forth, crunching snow. "But Phillip is our rock. He's our direct link to God and we should be happy to... to provide for him, for our church, and for the Lord. Ashleigh couldn't handle the pressure, I guess."

Tehlor steeled her expression. Dread pooled in her gut. "Provide what?"

"Expansion," Amy said as if Tehlor should've known. She furrowed her brow. "Abundance."

Jesus Christ. She swallowed and gave a curt nod, forcing a smile. It made sense and it didn't. She remembered how Phillip had touched her in the foyer, so simply, so easily. Remembered how Rose had commanded the women in the kitchen. *Of course.* She held out her hand, asking for the vape. Amy passed it to her with a sly grin. *You're cattle*, she thought, disgusted. *Breeding stock.*

"Thanks," she said and handed the vape back to Amy.

"I'm glad we met, Tehlor. I know Haven can be a lot—I can be a lot—but it's nice to have a friend."

"You have plenty of friends. I'm glad we met, too, though. I needed to get out of the house."

A small, hopeless laugh lurched from Amy's mouth, sudden and then smothered. "Well, c'mon, let's go make some s'mores," she chirped, stepping back into who she'd been in the kitchen, at the metaphysical shop. Lively and sweet, faithful and unwavering. The Haven good girl.

Tehlor followed her around the side of the house and through the gate, closing it behind her. Firelight licked snowy patio furniture and danced on the frost spread across the yard. Shadows stretched away from ankles, jilting with each step and casual movement. Rose clutched a refilled wine glass, swathed in a wool coat with polished buttons, and Phillip laughed as he speared a marshmallow, nodding at something one of the other men said. Lincoln stood with Daniel. Their conversation appeared tense. Or maybe emotional. Tehlor watched the pair out of the corner of her eye, tracking Lincoln's solemn nod and Daniel's heavy sigh. Definitely emotional. Lincoln swatted Daniel on the back—*men*—and said something that made Daniel pinch the bridge of his nose.

"Looks like our husbands get along," Amy said, nudging Tehlor with her elbow. "C'mon, let's have a treat—hey, hey! Oh, those look dee-licious. Jackie, can you hand me one?"

The Haven parishioners clustered in small, obvious alliances. Women huddled together, coupled or as a trio, and men stood apart from them, talking amongst themselves. Tehlor continued collecting information, tidbits she could exploit later. One of Phillip's friends walked with a well-masked limp. The redhead who'd asked about her tattoo traded nervous glances with a man who wasn't her husband. Rose watched like a wolf surveying sheep, standing near the small bonfire.

The second Tehlor relaxed enough to step into the bonfire's warmth and properly case the house, she noticed movement through the slider. It was quick. A sudden flash, but a blur far too familiar to disregard. *Don't you fuckin' do it.* She kept her face forward but slid her eyes toward the glass door that led to the kitchen. Gunnhild, who had jostled Tehlor's purse from atop the table, rounded the corner and scampered into the hall. *Jesus, Mary, and fucking Joseph.*

Amy stepped up next to her, holding a sleeve of graham crackers. "Tehlor, do you want—"

"Where's the powder room?" Tehlor interrupted. She flashed a tight grin. "Sorry. Yes, I do want one, but I have to pee first."

"Oh, it's down the hall on the left. I can show—"

"No, no," she blabbed, flapping her hands. "Make your s'more. I'll be right back."

Tehlor ignored Lincoln's curious look and darted inside, carefully navigating the kitchen tile on her snow-slicked heels. She kicked her purse aside as she entered the hall, frantically searching for a fleshy tail and listening for the pitter-patter of paws.

"*Gunnhild*," she hissed, whispering. "Gunnhild, what the *fuck?*"

A squeak sounded from the staircase.

Tehlor slipped. Her ankle folded and she caught herself on the wall, reaching for one shoe and then the other. She abandoned her wet heels and pulled up her dress, seething as she climbed the staircase. At the top, she spotted Gunnhild hopping down the narrow hall.

"Where the hell are you going?" She snuck a glance over her shoulder before barreling down the hall after her familiar. "Hey, Gunnnild, stop—*Gunnhild!*"

The rat halted in front of a plain, eggshell-colored door in the center of the hall, flanked by an empty bedroom and positioned across from a bathroom with a spotless vanity. Tehlor mumbled as she strode forward—*you little shit* and *come here* and *you're gonna get us kicked out* and *what are you even doing* and *you're like a drunk girl at a bar*—but paused mid-crouch. Her open hand hovered above Gunnhild, who sniffed at the bottom of the door, and her heart seized.

There was something about fear, something animal and grounding, that never failed to impress her. No one liked being afraid, but she appreciated it. How adrenaline shot through her like an upturned bottle, spilling in her stomach. How she couldn't speak, or move, or do much of anything when it first arrived. How fear took her by the neck and said *look*.

Two skinny, battered fingers slid beneath the door and curled, showing bloodied cuticles and bitten nails. Gunnhild sniffed the bony digits. The person—*thing*—on the other side of the door stretched its fingers outward, reaching.

Hauntings didn't show themselves outright. Ghosts, ghouls, and demons cloaked their energy behind innate humanness. Anger, joy, reverence, pain. Spiritual entities used the animalistic patterns at the forefront of unsuspecting minds to cut through corporeal spaces without being noticed.

But this is no haunting, she thought and took a small step backward. The air thinned and crackled. Her lungs ached, but she refused to gasp, rejecting the instinct to panic.

The person behind the door spoke, their voice overlayed like a warped recorder. Many people, many things. "I can smell you."

Tehlor snatched Gunnhild up from the floor and cradled her close to her chest.

"You know not what you do." Lilting, scratchy tones. Like a dove, like a woman, man, bear, toddler. "Pray with me, child of the Æsir."

"Who are you?" Tehlor asked, taking another step backward.

Clammy, invisible hands slid around her biceps, halting her in place. A chapped mouth scraped her cheek. Tehlor's lungs tightened. Sour blood, like roadkill in summer, perfumed the air. She reached for the magic churning inside her and thought *light*, thought *burn*, thought *get away, go, run*. Her heart raced. Fear choked her.

Whatever had manifested in the Haven house was not power, but something worse. The unmaking of it. Whatever surrounded her, whatever pressed itself to the backside of that door, was absent the stability of an earth-bound vessel. It was sticky, and brutal, and *wrong*.

"Come with me to the garden," the disembodied voice, mingling with noises she couldn't parse—wails, chitters, cries—whispered
against her ear.

She thrashed, stumbling sideways, swatting at the air.

The moment she broke away, everything went to hell. The person—thing, creature—on the other side of the door let out a shocking
scream. The fingers that'd reached out from beneath the bottom of the
door disappeared. Fists, feet, or shoulders smashed against the wood,
jostling the lock. Knuckles rapped and pounded. A horrible wail filled
the house.

"Let me out," someone shouted. A girl, maybe. "Please, let me
out—they're making me do it, please, *please*—I'm Sophia!"

Tehlor couldn't move. Her fear became something else. Terror,
enlightenment.

We're too late, she thought, miserably. *Fuck, we're too late.*

"Sophia De'voreaux!" Her shrill voice careened through the hall.
Fingernails scraped paint and wood. The doorknob rattled violent-
ly. Other sounds accompanied her voice—chirping birds, growling
beasts, ocean waves. "They're going to kill me; *they're going to kill
us—*"

"Tehlor!" Lincoln appeared—footsteps firm on the floor, hand a
comforting weight on her elbow—and yanked her aside.

Silence, so abrupt, so unnatural, snapped into place. Sophia's voice
disappeared. Like a television had been unplugged. As if Tehlor had
been pulled from one reality into another.

She swallowed, righting herself, and tucked Gunnhild into her coat
pocket.

All those sounds, the shouting, banging, and crying were immediately replaced with eerie nothing. She stared at the door, flicking her

attention from its center, then to the knob, and finally to the sliver at the bottom where a shadow crept back and forth.

"Get me out of here," she said, so low she hadn't realized she'd spoken. Her throat was scratchy and raw. She tasted iron.

"You were *screaming*," he hissed, tightening his hold on her arm. "What the hell were you thinking—"

She whipped toward him, eyes wide and unblinking. Her mouth pressed tightly, and she shook her head, unable to form a single thought except *no* and *we're done* and *this is not what we signed up for, this is not what I want.* The thought was not her own, though. It was an intruder, flitting through her skull, unwelcome and alien.

"I wasn't," she snapped under her breath, then again, gaze locked with his. "*I wasn't.*"

"Is everything okay?" Amy asked, appearing at the top of the stairs.

Lincoln eyed her carefully. His attention sharpened as if he'd realized something, as if he *knew*.

Tehlor peeked around him and tried to smile. "Yes, of course. Sorry, I got a little turned around."

From behind the door, a weak voice, hushed and timid, snuck through.

"Help me," Sophia whispered. "Please, please, please—"

"That's enough," Amy snapped, switching her attention to the bedroom. She turned to stone, expression hardening, eyes glazing over, hot with anger. Tehlor hadn't thought she was capable of such fury. It was hatred. The barbed, wicked, practiced kind. Rage long in making.

Tehlor startled. Lincoln did, too, but he kept his composure and cleared his throat.

"Sorry," Amy said, sighing through it. Her voice lightened and laughter chimed, porcelain in her mouth. "She's a handful. C'mon, let's get you two back downstairs." She opened her arm, gesturing toward the staircase. Her smile split into a grin.

"Amy," Tehlor deadpanned. Her practiced guise fell, and she furrowed her brow, waiting for the woman who'd puffed on a vape pen in the snow to appear again. *You're not completely delusional, are you?* Tehlor clung to useless hope. *There's still a chance for you, right?* "Is she okay?"

Amy tilted her head. Her grin dropped. "Of course," she said, firmly, unwavering. "'I urge you, brothers and sisters, to offer your bodies as a living sacrifice, holy and pleasing to God.'" She nodded slowly and stared at Tehlor. Her fingertips twitched, curling into a white-knuckled fist. "And with Adam's rib, she was made, as I was, as you were. So, Sophia is being held in quiet contemplation before her ascendence at the revival. There's nothing to be worried about, Tehlor. This is all predetermined, you know." She made another insistent wave toward the stairs. "S'more time," she chirped, shimmying her shoulders.

Muffled weeping erupted on the other side of the locked door.

Amy hushed the hidden girl. It was a sharp, violent sound, like a strong faucet or an abusive mother.

Tehlor walked forward, flanked by Lincoln, and tried not to flinch when Amy set her delicate hand between her shoulder blades, rubbing reassuringly.

Crazy fuckin' Jesus freaks. She reached into her pocket and held onto Gunnhild. The rat stayed still, fuzzy nose twitching against her fingers.

Tehlor slowed on the staircase. Across the hall, the kitchen was crowded. She was met with the entire Haven cult waiting, silent and attentive. People stood shoulder to shoulder, watching her with an intensity she hadn't known for many, many years. Impossible judgment. Scrutiny so fine-tuned she felt it in the soles of her feet and in her sweat-slicked palms. No one moved, no one spoke. Like soldiers, the congregation stood at the ready, devastatingly quiet.

For the first time that night, Tehlor felt Lincoln's body clench, anxiety locking around each muscle.

Once they stepped into the hall, Amy moved aside, positioned between the parishioners and Tehlor. She smiled, waiting with the rest.

"The Lord will keep her," Tehlor said because it was the only reasonable thing she could possibly do. *Give them obedience. Show them you're on their side. Be agreeable.*

Amy beamed. Satisfaction slackened Phillip's face, but Rose looked entirely unimpressed. Still, the house echoed her.

"The Lord will keep her," rang out, spoken in unison.

Tehlor steadied herself, willed her smile to stay sweet, and told her body to withstand the panic gracefully. *Don't let them see you afraid.* She closed her eyes, nodding along to the sound of fifty voices, and brought her thrift store crucifix to her mouth, kissing it. Lincoln pressed against her back, staying close. The heat of him sank through her clothes and a foolish, half-baked thought ran through her mind. *My vorðr would rip you all apart.* But she didn't know that for sure. Not anymore.

"Let's get you home," Lincoln said.

"Leaving already?" Rose asked. She eased from the crowd and gave Tehlor a quick once over. "I put your shoes by the door."

Tehlor swallowed hard. "Oh, thank you."

Her spindly hands landed below Tehlor's elbows and swept upward, caging her there, holding her captive. Rose met her eyes and Tehlor knew a searching look like that. It was the same expression cops, and priests, and savvy shop clerks wore. Suspicion shielded by strength.

"Your baptism will be beautiful. Drowning your past, emerging new..." Rose said and centered Tehlor's crucifix overtop of her high-necked dress. "It's the godliest thing we can do, I think. Give ourselves to fate and let the Lord decide if we're worthy."

"Holy Father speaks through you, Rose. I'm just happy to be here."

Rose's smile sharpened. She leaned closer, pressing a chaste kiss to Tehlor's cheek. "And as the Lord kept us, we too shall keep you."

The hair on Tehlor's nape stood. She brushed her lips across Rose's cheek, mimicking her, and then stepped backward, allowing Lincoln to reach out and clasp Phillip's hand. They said their goodbyes through manufactured smiles and fake laughter, waving joyfully as they slipped through the front door.

Once they were across the street, Tehlor quickened her pace, clutching her heels and purse in one hand and fumbling for the handle on the passenger's door with the other. She tossed the keys at Lincoln. The frozen ground left her bare feet numb and chapped. She rubbed them together and shivered, pulling Gunnhild out of her coat pocket.

Lincoln climbed into the driver's seat. Anger tightened his handsome face. "What the fuck was that?"

"It's over. We're done, we're packin' it in."

"What?"

"They already used it—the breath, the relic, *whatever*—can you drive, please?" She flung her free hand toward the slowly defrosting windshield. "It's too late. There's literally nothing to steal, so we're done. We're not going back—"

"Tehlor, c'mon. There's no way—"

"You weren't there," she snapped. Gunnhild squeaked, startled by her shrill voice. Tehlor held the rat beneath her chin and mumbled an apology. "You didn't hear whatever they've got locked behind that door, okay?"

Lincoln stayed quiet. He faced forward in the seat and inhaled a long, deep breath, sighing thoughtfully.

The windshield cleared. He yanked on the gear shifter and hit the gas.

Gideon passed by in swathes of glittering white and dark brick, naked trees and black skies. Tehlor chewed her lip. Fear influenced her the way it did most mid-sized hunters. Like a fox, she assessed her prey carefully, silent and smart. And like a fox, she knew better than to continue a hunt after she'd been bested. Rose was a grizzly with an army of sharp-toothed minions at her disposal. Going up against her and Haven was a death wish. And that thing. *That thing.* She still felt its breath on her ear. Still felt the cold dread creeping along her insides.

Tehlor had reached for power, had called to her magic, but she hadn't been able to summon anything more than panic.

Forgive me, she thought, calling out to Hel. *For weakness prevailed when strength was needed.*

"I think you're overreacting," Lincoln said, steady and too calm.

"If you try to make me feel crazy about this, I'll get crazy. I'll get real fuckin' crazy, Lincoln," she bit out, glaring at him. "Whatever they've got in that house, it's not anything I've dealt with before. Witchcraft, potions, curses, sacrifices, spirit boards, I can deal with that shit. But this was..." She pictured the battered fingers curved around the bottom of the door, beckoning her. "This was some exorcist stuff, okay? Straight Linda Blair shit."

He guided the truck into the driveway and parked, nodding along as she spoke. His two-toned eyes remained soft yet attentive, but his mouth curved into a smile, expression strung between confidence and something else. Excitement. Hunger.

"Not anything *you've* dealt with," he said, unbuckling his seatbelt.

"Right, I forgot, you're a demonologist who definitely has experience handling one of the most powerful religious relics rumored to exist," she deadpanned.

"I'm a demonologist who definitely has experience dealing with literal demons," he shot back and came around the car to open her door. "Now tell me what happened."

Tehlor slid out of the truck and walked inside, relaying the encounter at the Haven house to Lincoln as effectively as she could. She set Gunnhild down, draped her coat and purse over the back of the couch, and dropped her shoes. Lincoln didn't speak. He listened, tipping his head as she paced in the living room, striding from the couch to the kitchen, then pausing to reach into the fridge and crack open a beer. She guzzled the cold, crisp beverage while he took off his labradorite necklace. He shook out his wolfish head and scratched behind one fuzzy ear, yawning wide to show rows of sharp, pointed teeth.

"So, you think Phillip and Rose are trying to get people pregnant," Lincoln deadpanned.

"The wives, yeah. I think they're building, like, an incest army."

Lincoln mouthed *incest army* and shook his head. "Which would make it a sex cult."

Tehlor batted at the air, shooing the idea. "Yeah, sure, that."

"And they've already given the Breath of Judas to this girl?" Lincoln asked.

"Sophia, yeah."

"And she's Amy's sister?"

"That's what Amy told me."

"Well, her husband cheated on her," he said, nodding at Tehlor's raised brows. "He's real torn up about it, but he's positive the revival bath'll set things straight."

"He told you that? After meeting you for, what, five minutes?"

"You'd be surprised what people will tell you when you pretend to be on their side," he said.

True. Tehlor wrinkled her nose. "Okay, but what does Daniel cheating on his wife have to do with..." She narrowed her eyes. *Oh.* "You think he fucked her sister."

"I think he fucked her sister," Lincoln repeated, setting his palms on the breakfast bar. He licked his canine, pink tongue darting over slick, white bone. "I'm not questioning whatever you experienced, okay? But what if we can get this girl on our side? If they're using her as a vessel for the Breath of Judas then we can steal *her*, can't we?"

"You're talking about kidnapping a person. Like, a living, breathing person—"

"Who is being kept against her will in a church safehouse by a militia-sex-cult," he said, adding weight to each word. "Doubt she'll mind hanging out with us for a while."

She listed her head, considering. "You're not wrong, but where do we even go from there? Do we try to get the magic out of her? Exorcise her? Convince her to work for us? C'mon, that's messy."

"Sure, yeah."

"*Yeah?* To what, exactly? Getting the magic out of her, exorcising her, or—"

"It's a mess," he snapped. He rolled his eyes and huffed out an exasperated breath. "But since when have you cared about messy?"

Tehlor sipped her beer and shrugged.

Lincoln walked into the kitchen.

"You're not scared of shit," he said, inching closer, backing her against the counter. Playfulness edged into his voice. "You're vicious, and powerful, and way too fuckin' confident for your own good." He slid his hand around her neck, angling her face upward. Her heart skipped, but he kept his grip loose, thumb following her jaw. "Don't let some glorified worship band get in your head, all right? We go to the revival, we find the girl, and we get out. The end."

Attentiveness seared her. She found his wrist with her free hand, closing her palm around his pulse. Weeks ago, he'd held her in a similar fashion against the bathroom wall, snarling about murder and deception. Right then, like that, she noticed the warmth in his eyes, how he loomed over her like a bodyguard, and smiled despite the uncertainty bundled in her chest. The radical, reckless part of her that'd bargained with a goddess to bring him back to life sat in direct opposition to the barbed, defensive part of her that couldn't fathom what might happen if she lost him. Love was a word she refused to use. It was too soon, too fresh, and love was too unpredictable to trust.

But Tehlor was obsessed with him. Hyper-fixated on what he did to her, how he influenced her. She clung to the rich, heady desire boiling in her stomach. Chased the devotion they'd mutually ignored and exploited. She wanted to be his *source*. His point of contention. The thing that made him weak and selfish.

Because Lincoln Stone had unburied something wicked and wrong inside her. Something she couldn't deny. And she desperately wanted to do the same to him.

"It's never that simple," she murmured.

"It is when you're us."

She finished her beer and set the can on the counter. "And if it goes wrong?"

Laughter purred in his throat. "For their sake, I hope it doesn't."

CHAPTER TEN

T EHLOR DREAMED OF BONE and ice.

After an evening spent arguing revival logistics in the living room, she'd wordlessly pulled Lincoln upstairs into her bedroom and tucked herself against him. Despite her racing mind, she'd drifted easily, but sometime in the night, her peaceful, dreamless sleep evaporated. Black sand stretched beneath her bare feet, morphing into golden wheat, then vibrant grass. Thunder cracked and lightning splintered. When the clouds opened, red pelted her naked skin.

Drums pounded from somewhere in the distance, thrumming through her like a second heartbeat. The world moved slowly as if she'd stepped into a place where time lost its footing. Skeletons littered the beach—antlers, skulls, vertebrae—and the rain tasted coppery and biotic. Tehlor tried to walk toward the water, but the tide retreated, flowing backward, upward, until the foam and waves became a shifting, living thing. When she blinked, the sand beneath her feet became snow, and the sea-made creature took a familiar shape.

"Chainbreaker, chosen by Hel," the black wolf said. His mighty jaws did not move, but Fenrir's voice shook through her. "Be wise, child of old. Even gods lie; even the faithful face betrayal."

Tehlor opened her mouth to speak but her lungs were empty, her voice gone.

"Call for me, Völva, and be vigilant. The mighty kneel before no one."

Fenrir's breath hit her face. He was a hulking, mountainous beast with eyes like cinders. The ground trembled beneath his paws and behind him where the ocean continued to thrash, scales, fins, and teeth speared the horizon. *Hafgúa, sea-serpent, wrecker of ships.* Lightning illuminated the sky. In her peripheral, winged soldiers dotted the blackness, and tall, armored beings stood on a rocky spire. *Oh, how I've chased you*, she thought, surrounded by godkin. *The things I've done to find you.*

"The things you'll do to be kept," Fenrir snarled. He opened his mouth and closed his jaws around her.

Teeth punctured. Her limbs loosened. Flesh ripped.

Tehlor came to with a shout. She reached beneath her pillow and grasped the handle of her lipstick-shaped pocketknife, swinging it toward the shadow.

Something warm halted her, snatching her wrist in a firm grip.

She blinked, swallowing to wet her scratchy throat, and waited for the dream to disintegrate. Her blurry vision sharpened. The room stopped spinning. Lincoln, upright and propped on one elbow, shook with exertion and craned away from the blade snug against his Adam's apple.

"Drop it," he rumbled.

Tehlor immediately opened her hand. The knife thumped on the bed between them.

"Bad dream," she blurted.

"I can see that."

"Sorry," she said, swallowing hard.

Lincoln kept hold of her wrist. In the dark, his sharp, animalistic features deepened. His ears twitched, perked at attention, and his damp nose wiggled. "You good?"

She nodded. "I need to do something."

He let her go. "Like?"

Tehlor couldn't describe the urge permeating inside her, as if someone had planted a thought—not her own, not homegrown—and demanded the completion of a task. Maybe it was a leftover directive from the dream; maybe Fenrir had truly granted her an audience. She didn't know. But what she *did* know was how insistently the thought tugged at her, coaxing her out of bed and across the room where she fumbled on the dresser for her cheap crucifix.

"Give me that knife," she said, holding her hand out.

Lincoln slapped the tool into her palm. "Don't do anything stupid."

She hushed him and set the tip of the blade against the backside of the cross. The inscription was hard to carve, but she did her best, etching each tiny line of the Sowilō rune into the necklace. She finished and set the knife on the dresser, feeling across the carved mark with her thumb. *Chainbreaker*. Fenrir's gravelly voice filled her mind. In the old poems and texts, paranoid godkin had bound Fenrir with chains and rope and left him to fester, enraged and deceived, until Ragnarök. If the great wolf deemed her *chainbreaker* then she would take his blessing and run with it.

"Rumor has it, Aleister Crowley and Anton LaVey based their sex rituals off seiðr," she said, fastening the crucifix around her neck.

"When they consumed feminine flesh and strapped people to tables, they were following in my ancestors' footsteps. Wild, huh?"

"That powerful men exploited ancient rituals to get laid? Pretty standard, to be honest."

"That occultism is older than Christianity." She climbed onto the bed, sliding her thighs around his hips. "Modesty, submission, obedience. That's new world shit. Worship used to be violent and sexy and weird."

"*Weird*," Lincoln echoed, laughing under his breath. "What're we doin', Tehlor? Talk to me."

"Pleasing the gods," she said.

Tehlor placed her palm on his chest. He sank into the bed, allowing her to guide him, and trailed his hands along her thighs, hips, settling just beneath her ribcage. Her naked body thrummed from the dream, clinging to magic and godhood. She still felt Fenrir's teeth clamped around her, splitting her skin, and the blood-rain bouncing off her forehead. She reached for his muzzle and slipped her thumb into his mouth, pressing the pad of her finger against his long, curved fang.

Pain, the sharp, brittle kind, bloomed in her hand. She pulled away and smeared the blood over the rune she'd etched onto her crucifix. Lincoln made a worried noise, like a growl but weaker, and licked his teeth. The magic strung between them pulled tighter, humming like a plucked bowstring. Tehlor remembered the ghostly hands around her arms, the ethereal voice tempting her at the Haven house, and Sophia's awful scream. She remembered the presence of *nothing*. How power unmade itself in the presence of whatever she'd stumbled upon.

But you will not unmake me, she thought. *You will not take what's mine.*

Lincoln fumbled for his necklace on the nightstand. Tehlor leaned over him, flattened her hand over his arm, and trapped him against the bed.

"Patience," she cooed.

"Be reasonable."

"You embarrassed?" She ran her free hand over his snout and cheek, framing his ear with her fingers.

Beneath her, Lincoln pressed himself between her thighs.

"Tryin' to be courteous," he said through gritted teeth.

Tehlor sank down on his cock. She saw glimpses of herself through his eyes—pupils misted over, red streaked on her sternum where the cross bumped against her skin, mouth slightly parted—and focused on magic, on chaos, on truth. She smiled at the ill-restrained leap of his hips. Breathed deeply, mindfully as Lincoln's lashes fluttered and his scarred chest reddened.

"Be honest," she dared.

Lincoln sighed. "Didn't think you'd want to kiss me like this."

She leaned closer, riding him slow and hard, and pressed her mouth to the side of his muzzle. She kissed his face until his ears drooped and his grip tightened on her waist. Lovingly ran her lips across his bony nose, pressed a kiss between his eyes, and didn't stop as he fumbled for his necklace again, didn't move away when he let her go, fastening the magical gemstone around his neck.

"I made you in the image of the true gods," she whispered, nuzzling his cheek.

Lincoln kissed her as the cloaking spell settled. She felt his sharp teeth on her lips before they were gone, heard the growl flutter in his throat before the sound eased into a soft moan. She thought of Fenrir, and magic, and godkin. Imagined the beat of Valkyrie wings, the clash of iron, the arctic sea rushing over black sand.

"Brave little witch," he whispered, gently, like a lover, rocking his hips in time with hers.

Glory, she thought, gasping against Lincoln's mouth. *Glory, glory, glory.*

The revival started at seven o'clock.

Family-friendly picnic areas draped the wilderness park in a false skin. But deeper, the Gideon Preserve's perfectly manicured trails and popular campgrounds faded. Trees leaned together, shielding outsiders from the mossy forest floor, turning the state-protected area into a place for illicit affairs. Drug use, illegal bonfires, séances, cultish gatherings. Anyone with a score to settle or a spell to cast knew to wander past the signs—WARNING: THICK BRUSH AHEAD and CAUTION: LIMITED RANGER ACCESS—and follow overgrown paths toward unknown rivers and unnamed meadows.

Lincoln drove the clunky truck down a dirt road. The headlights striped tree trunks and shot through the blackness. Icicles glinted like eyes in the pitch. Tehlor held Gunnhild beneath her chin, stroking the rat with two fingers. It'd been a silent, tense drive, but when Tehlor finally opened her mouth to say *I hope we're not lost*, she stopped, catching a glimmer in the distance. As they cruised closer, the image solidified. Candles on stilts lined a skinny road that led into the belly of the woods. A cross faced outward from the mouth of the path, holding up a sign that read: *Rejoice for the Lord on High is Here! The Blessed Begin Anew!*

"Park the truck, join the flock, find the girl," Lincoln said, reciting the first half of their plan in a calm, steady tone. "I distract the congregation, you take the girl, we meet at this trailhead and call it a night. In the morning, we regroup with Haven and join the search party. Play the part, put on a show."

Tehlor nodded. It was a good, simple plan. "And if something goes wrong?"

"We improvise."

"And if something goes *really* wrong?"

Lincoln turned to face her. His strange, mismatched eyes—lupine and a little too animal to be wholly familiar—narrowed playfully.

"Then we kill them," he said, shrugging. "Leave their bodies to freeze overnight, take the girl back to the townhouse, and either find a way to extract the Breath of Judas or figure out how to use her power."

"You're serious." She let her eyes slip shut and inhaled a long, deep breath through her nose. Gunnhild squeaked restlessly, squirming between her palms. "Let's hope this shit works. I survived juvi, but I'm *way* too pretty for prison." She shot him a cold glance. "And you are too, so."

He laughed in his throat.

The truck lurched over uneven ground, creaking as they followed the twinkling candles.

If things went wrong—*they won't, they can't*—Tehlor had very little room for improvisation. She took a mental inventory of her body. The black jumpsuit she'd chosen was sleek and easy to move in. Her wool coat was heavy enough to keep the cold out but fit snugly and didn't make a sound. She'd taken Lincoln's advice and worn boots. Easier to run in; inflicted more pain if necessary. She shifted her foot, pressing her shin against the sheathed knife stashed behind the zipper.

A small sliver of her couldn't shake what she'd stumbled upon at the Haven house—the ghostly voice rippling through her skull, the rancid breath on her neck. Instinct told her to turn around, to let it go, to drop the hunt and find something safer to chase. Fenrir's warning squirmed inside her. *Even the faithful face betrayal.* She glanced sideways at Lincoln. Remembered his heavy gaze locked with her own, his hands on her face, holding her tenderly as she went to pieces in his lap. How he'd reached between them, touched where they were connected, and brought slick fingers to his mouth, tasting unwieldy sex magic. How after, when the ritual was done and Tehlor had barely caught her breath, he'd turned her over, wrapped his hand around her throat, and fucked her hard and fast. Held her impossibly close. Made a mess of her and said *that's it, baby. Good girl. Say my name.*

And she had, like a prayer, laughing and moaning.

"You're staring," he said.

"If you fuck me over, I'll castrate you. You know that, right?"

Lincoln laughed again, guiding the truck around a thorny bush. "I'm well aware."

"I'm serious, Lincoln."

"Uh huh, because you weren't thinking about taking the Breath of Judas for yourself, using it to make me bend the knee, and cashing in on an actual *slave?* That never crossed your mind?" He stole a glance at her, brow furrowed, lips parted. "C'mon, I don't fuck where I shit. I wouldn't have—"

"Excuse me? Not to be a bummer, babe, but you have a well-documented history of fucking where you shit—"

Lincoln stomped on the brake and shoved the gear shifter into *park.* He whipped toward her and held out his hand, asking for Gunnhild.

When she didn't hand her over, he heaved a sigh, curling his fingers impatiently. Tehlor set her familiar in his palm and watched him place the rat on the dash, stroking her head with his pointer finger. Once Tehlor's palms were free, he seized them, snatching her up in a two-handed grasp. Like that, facing each other in mock devotion, Lincoln met her eyes and brought her knuckles to his mouth.

"I could've done this job without you," he said. Gentleness wrapped around each word. "It would've been easier, more efficient, quicker—"

"Bullshit."

"Tehlor," he warned.

She went quiet, waiting.

"I could've taken the Breath of Judas for myself. I'm meaner than you—" He snared her with an impatient glare, halting her before she could speak. She closed her mouth. "—I'm ruthless; you're cunning. I'm straightforward; you're a goddamn weasel. I could've killed you weeks ago. Could've put you in the wall where you found me." He nodded as if to say *it's true* and it was. "If this whole thing was on me, I'd poison the baptism water, watch them all choke to death, knock the girl unconscious, and kill whoever got in my way. It'd take ten minutes. Maybe twenty."

"Then why..." She stopped. Her lips squirmed and she held her breath, allowing him to finish.

"Because you're smart," he whispered, squeezing her small hands. "You're patient. You move like a shadow. You're persistent and savvy and fierce, but you don't flaunt it. It's for *you*—power, magic, faith, it's all yours. You don't care about status, immortality, leaving a mark... None of that shit matters to you. You belong entirely to yourself, and I envy that."

That's not true, she thought. *I've tricked you, Lincoln Stone.*

Tehlor tilted her head, studying his strong bones and timid smile. *Envy.* What a strange thing for him to say. She blushed horribly.

Lincoln touched his lips to her knuckles again, resting his mouth there. "You can choose to believe me or not. That's up to you. But I need you to trust me. At this point, the bar is on the fuckin' floor, okay? You can at least give me that."

"Fine." She tucked everything he'd said close to her heart and steeled her expression, nodding curtly.

"Do I need to bring up the slave stuff again or—"

"No, I got it," she blurted, exhaling hard.

"Good." He kissed her.

She kept her eyes open. He did, too. Their lips met, briefly, firmly, and Tehlor's chest constricted.

"Good," she echoed. "Give me my rat back. Let's go."

Lincoln scooped Gunnhild up and handed her to Tehlor, then yanked the gearshift into *drive*.

In the rearview mirror, headlights blinked on the road behind them, following the candlelit path. About a mile in, the trees gave way to a large inlet and the revival came into view.

A large, decorative gazebo filled the center of the meadow. Chic, boho string lights hung from wooden beams, evenly draped from each corner, and fastened in the center of the structure. Other, smaller gazebos were interconnected, creating segmented spaces where people moved about, helping themselves to coffee in one area, praying in another, and swaying with their hands above their heads as an acoustic band played in the largest. Tehlor noticed the baptism station immediately, staring intently at the trough near the back of the closest gazebo.

Cars and trucks bracketed the snowy path on either side of the road. Lincoln parked next to a Land Cruiser, so new it didn't have plates.

"Stay in there," Tehlor said to Gunnhild and slipped the spotted rat into her purse. "I'm serious. These people will kill you, okay? *Stay*."

Gunnhild nestled into a scarf bundled at the bottom of the bag and wiggled her nose. Tehlor closed the purse and slung it over her shoulder, pausing to check herself in the visor mirror. Dusty rose lipstick, mascara, eyebrow gel. She smoothed her palms over the modest bun secured at her nape, and nodded at her reflection. The driver's side door creaked open.

"You good?" Lincoln asked.

Your ancestors conquered the land and the sea, she told herself. *You are chainbreaker, blessed by Fenrir, child of the north, descendent of shield-maidens.* She slid out of the truck and shut the door. *Take no shit, bitch.* "Yeah, let's go."

Walking into the Haven madness felt like wading into glacier water. She cleared her throat and took Lincoln's hand, assuming her role as devoted wife, eager convert, newborn Christian. A few women from the cookout waved. Daniel stood with Phillip near the band, nodding slowly as the pastor spoke. Newcomers rambled in tongues—lilting, sporadic sounds coaxed from open throats and chittering mouths—and gospel-style Lord Huron filled the air. Tehlor chewed on the inside of her cheek and squeezed Lincoln's palm, casting a cautious glance from one gazebo to the next.

The area beyond the revival was bathed in thick darkness. No trails pierced the treeline. No other outlets; no other escape routes. One way in. One way out. Moonlight skirted the meadow, silver and muted, only peeking through when the cloud cover drifted. *Perfect*, Tehlor thought. It was a masterful trap. Easily guarded, easily hidden, easily contained. Leaving would be tricky but with a big enough distraction...

"Tehlor, hi," Amy exclaimed, sidestepping a person with their hands held high, swaying to worship music. Her knee-length taupe skirt hugged her legs, and a black puffy vest was zipped to her chin. She reached for Tehlor, taking her by the wrist, and turned to Lincoln. "You should join the boys," she said, nodding toward Pastor Phillip. "They'll get you ready to be anointed."

Anointed. Tehlor made the shape of the word but stayed silent.

Lincoln watched Amy closely. He nodded and let go of Tehlor's hand.

"Be careful with my wife," he said, closing his blue eye in a quick wink.

Tehlor watched Lincoln walk away, suddenly struck with the sick, exciting thrill of being separated. Of knowing their plan was officially in motion. She turned toward Amy and offered a practiced smile.

"Do I get to be anointed?" Tehlor asked.

Amy batted her gloved hand in the air. "No, no, that's only for those in service of the household. He'll be anointed and then he'll assist with your baptism."

"What do you mean?"

She quirked her head, amused. "Oh, well, he's your husband. So, you're in service to him through God which means he's in service to God through you, but since he's the head of the house he has the authority to step in and assist with your baptism. Adam and Eve. Strength and sensitivity; provider and provided for—you know the drill. By his hands, you'll be washed anew." She grinned, rubbing Tehlor's arm reassuringly. "Me and Daniel are doing the same thing, don't be nervous."

Batshit. Tehlor tried to relax her jaw, but her smile cracked. She wanted to take Amy by the shoulders and give her a good shake. *Wake up, bitch*. She wanted to take her out for a cocktail and lean in close over a shitty, stained bar. *They're playing you. Rose would gut you in a heartbeat if it kept her in control.* But she swallowed instead and nodded along. When she curled her arm around Amy's elbow, the other woman hummed appreciatively.

"So, last night..." Tehlor paused, inching closer as Amy guided them toward a coffee station in the corner of the prayer gazebo.

"Don't worry about that." Amy huffed out a sigh and shook her head. She pursed her lips and untangled from Tehlor, busying her hands with paper cups and an insulated coffee dispenser. "I know it's kind of weird, okay? But Sophia is serving a greater purpose. Her transgressions are forgivable." Each word skipped like a stone in her mouth. "She'll atone with Holy Father and make right with her heart."

"And what about the..." Tehlor made a show of looking left and then right, and leaned closer, shielding a secret. "The Breath of—"

Amy hushed her through a giddy smile. "Oh, wait 'til you see," she whispered. Her tone shifted, suddenly slick with anticipation. *She's so sure,* Tehlor thought, miserably. *She's in too deep.* "Here we are, turning malice into miracles. Planting seeds. Ushering life into lifeless places."

Deep in Tehlor's spirit, where her hunger for power met old, decaying grief, where her past curdled and she yearned for womanhood, friendship, and safety, she hoped Amy might blink awake. Might shake off the spell and come to her senses. She felt like a drunk bitch in a bar, staring at her doe-eyed friend in the bathroom. *He's garbage, this is stupid, you're better than this.* And watching said friend walk out anyway. Right into danger, right into a lie.

Tehlor exhaled, pretending to be relieved. "You heard her, though, right? Your sister. You heard her last night when—"

"When she embarrassed me in front of the entire congregation? Yeah, I heard her. She's always been like that, you know. So over-dramatic. I mean, c'mon, she's in *atonement*, she's reflecting on her decisions, she's the chosen vessel. A lot of us would love to be in her shoes."

Chosen vessel. She tried to smile and took the coffee Amy handed her.

"Vikings believed in sacrifices, right? It's Old Testament stuff," Amy said, nonchalantly, and shrugged. "What we're doing here, the souls we're saving tonight, it's all by *his* design." She pointed at the top of the gazebo. "Those who are chosen will answer the call. They'll be fruitful—*we'll* be fruitful—and the Lord will keep us."

"The Lord will keep us," Tehlor said, forcing confidence into her voice.

Amy De'voreaux knew her sister was carrying the Breath of Judas. She knew Haven planned to kill her, she knew Rose and Phillip were leading the church down a violent, unsustainable path. Yet she *believed*, nonetheless. Death, murder, miracles. Amy subscribed to anything and everything blessed by the people who'd shamed her into compliance. For a brief, insignificant moment, Tehlor thought about starting her own cult.

It'd be easy, wouldn't it?

Candles dripped wax onto packed snow and Tehlor sipped the too-hot coffee, pushing the earthy flavor around in her mouth. She listened as Amy described the beginning of her day, talking in great detail about how *long* it'd taken to haul the materials into the preserve, prattling on about the setup—*it took, like forever* and *oh my gosh, I was dying for Starbies* and *I can't wait to be reborn*—but when she said those last two words, *be reborn*, Tehlor heard *die*. Hel's voice, hushed and rigid, coasted her left ear. *Die*, like a promise. *Die*, like it was something she should've known all along.

"What?" Tehlor asked.

"Be reborn," Amy repeated, flicking her hand toward the baptism trough. She bumped her shoulder against Tehlor's and lifted a brow. "We'll be miracles, you and me."

Fenrir, Tehlor silently prayed, *shackle my heart, turn my spine to steel.*

The music faded. Pastor Phillip took the microphone and stepped up onto the makeshift stage. People clapped and cheered, whistled and hooted. Tehlor scanned the space, glancing around shoulders and between attendees. Lincoln stood with Daniel and a few other men to the left of the stage. He seemed tense, almost. On alert. She glanced at wild-eyed, smiling faces, hands clasped tightly in predetermined prayer, and searched for inconsistencies, nervousness, caution. But everyone appeared at the ready, happy to be directed, grateful for the opportunity to stand in Phillip's presence. She startled when her eyes landed on Rose Whitman, standing opposite Lincoln on the other side of the small stage, staring back at her. Rose lifted her pointy chin. Her blonde hair was fastened into a tidy donut-bun, slick and perfect, and her unassuming off-white sweater-dress hugged the slight dent where her abdomen dove inward. She was the iconic Pastor's Wife. Beautifully polished, thin and unassuming, poised and venomous.

As Phillip spoke, Rose stepped forward, making her way through the crowd. She took mindful, easy steps, tracking Tehlor like a puma. Her steady gaze never wavered. Not when she set her hand on a shoulder, squeezing past, and not when she skirted her palm along someone's bicep, granting them a casual touch. Tehlor adjusted the strap on her purse, holding it tighter to her side.

Rose halted in front of Tehlor and said, "You made it."

"We did, yeah. This is beautiful." She opened her palm, signaling to the connected gazebos. Phillip preached about devotion, integrity, and commitment. Tehlor didn't know whether to break away from his wife and focus on the sermon or keep her attention on Rose. "Thank you again for including us."

"Are you ready to be reborn?" Rose tipped her head, letting her gaze fall to Tehlor's boots. She gave her a thoughtful once-over.

"I am, yeah. Of course."

"Good." Rose smiled. She reached into the small clutch roped over her shoulder and withdrew a small, green cutting. "Did you know some people consider this to be the most fertile tree on the planet? Depictions of Eden show it everywhere, growing tall and wide, providing shade for animals."

Tehlor focused on Rose, but Phillip's voice echoed. *Tonight, we face death! Tonight, we give ourselves to our almighty God! To he who made us in his image!* Beside her, Amy cupped her hand around her mouth and whooped.

Rose slid the branch into Tehlor's hot palm and continued. "Because if you planted that little thing, it'd grow roots and climb. Become entirely new. Even if its mother died, it would live."

Tehlor thumbed at the oval leaves. She thought the branch was wax at first, something bought in the home décor section at Hobby Lobby. But it was wilting, weak, and real.

"But other people think the willow is a bad omen. That it teaches the value of consequence," Rose said, folding her hand over Tehlor's, coaxing her fingers to curl around the willow cutting.

Phillip kept shouting. *Evil will not triumph tonight! The deceivers will turn thine own eyes toward heaven and be judged! Rejoice!*

Rose scraped her pink-painted fingernail across Tehlor's tattooed knuckles. "I think it's both, don't you? Life is nothing but a consequence until we make right with God. This—" She squeezed Tehlor's fist. "—is nothing but a stem until you plant it."

Tehlor pushed down the primal urge to call her magic to the surface. Anxiety pressed on her sternum. Her pulse ran rabbit-fast, and she could barely commit to a half-formed smile.

Since the first moment Rose Whitman had entered Moonstrike Nursery, Tehlor had sensed that something was inherently *off*. A grainy, malignant, disruptive energy was finely stitched into her very being, and Tehlor knew now that what she'd confused for standard rich-bitch, Bible-banging behavior was actually a well-oiled engine, gathering power, pushing her toward an empire.

People like Rose Whitman were the subjects of high-caliber profiles in popular magazines. They ran for office, had offshore accounts, and played a mean game of poker. They influenced, leeched, and ruined.

I underestimated you.

"Amen," Tehlor said and forced her faulty smile into a pretty grin. Magic buzzed in her wrists, elbows, ankles, deep in the pit of her, but she straightened her back and tucked the little willow behind her ear, then leaned in and kissed Rose on the cheek. "You're a willow, Rose. *You* provide shelter."

"And consequences," she said, low and private. She set her hand on the center of Tehlor's back and steered her toward the trough. "C'mon, acolyte. It's time for the baptisms."

Tehlor glanced over her shoulder, searching for familiarity.

Lincoln met her eyes, stoic and brave. His mouth made the shape of a single, terrifying command—*don't run*.

Chapter Eleven

"**B**APTISM IS A BLESSING," Phillip said.

The Haven congregation stood at attention, crowded around the shock tank. Among them, newcomers fidgeted nervously, giddy and itching for the miracle Pastor Phillip promised.

For days, Tehlor had researched revivals. She'd spent hours scouring YouTube, searching for video evidence and explanations. She'd watched long-winded documentaries on Hillsong, Peoples Temple, and the Branch Davidians, but she'd expected *more*. More expansion, more visionaries, more fresh blood. Surely Haven wanted to grow, right? She stared at the weird, steel trough branded with a fitness logo on its side. That was the whole point, wasn't it? Spread the good word; convert the nonbelievers—*whatever*. But this peculiar, strangled intimacy made her wonder about intent. Deliverables and sustainability.

A miracle was only defined by the people who witnessed it. The lack of new faces, the lack of *children*, frightened her.

"As most of you know, we came into possession of something monumentally important. A piece of our history gathered at a time of great deceit and protected under the guise of community well-being."

Phillip nodded, opening his arm toward the parked cars lining the treeline.

Lincoln squeezed through the small crowd and placed his hand on Tehlor's tailbone.

"This is it," he whispered, masking the information with a kiss to her temple. "I have a feeling I know what they're planning."

"Well, now would be a good time to spill the fuckin' tea," she hissed.

"You were right."

"*Obviously*. About which part?"

Lincoln hushed her and nodded in the direction Phillip pointed.

The string lights dimmed and vanished. Shadows stretched and flickered. Half-melted pillar candles gilded the snowy ground, and the preserve became an outdoor cathedral, silent except for the crunchy footsteps growing nearer. No one spoke. No one moved. The energy soured, turning the air like a day-old corpse. Tehlor leaned against Lincoln and clutched her purse.

You. Chills scaled her arms. Tehlor watched the pair come into view. Amy led a girl—nineteen, maybe twenty—by the elbow. *Sophia*. She was swathed in white, like a bride, wearing a long-sleeved dress with a high, high neckline. Her snow boots were cheap and tattered, clearly second-hand, and a head of beautiful, waist-length curls fell around her. Brunette, same as her sister. They shared a small nose and thin mouth.

"For she will keep the Lord, and the Lord will keep her. For she will carry what others cannot, and by the grace of God, defy death. Holder of old, conduit of deceit—you are the messenger, the lamb, and the light." Phillip raised his arm high, opening his palm toward the sky. "And the Lord will keep us."

The congregation spoke as one. "And the Lord will keep us."

Tehlor swallowed hard. Sophia's gaunt face held a ferocity she'd only ever seen in herself. Desperation, fear, rage. She stared straight ahead, mouth set tight, brow cinched with concentration, and trembled at Amy's side. No tears fell from her glassy eyes, but the thick sheen gave her away. Gave them all away.

"She's terrified," Tehlor whispered.

Lincoln hummed. "She's pissed," he corrected. "Feel that?"

"Yes," she spat. Of course, she felt it. Roiling, destabilizing magic. Power like a vacuum, suckling at any nearby source, shredding energy, unmaking hope.

Amy held Sophia in a white-knuckled grip. She smiled at Tehlor, though, as if they shared the same excitement, mania, *faith*. As if Tehlor had subscribed to whatever devotional Amy had mainlined for long enough to... to give up.

"Kimberly," Phillip said, offering a warm smile to a woman at the front of the gathering. "C'mon, darlin'."

A woman with a tidy blonde bob walked up to the trough. She placed one foot into the still water, shivered, then followed with the other. She cast a nervous smile around the group and sank down, submerged to her shoulders in the shock tank. Tehlor anticipated chatter, but the Haven congregation stayed entirely quiet. Everyone stared, electrified but completely still, like mannequins in a horror movie. Tehlor gripped Lincoln's hand.

Phillip stood at the top of the trough and touched the crown of Kimberly's head. "I hereby baptize you in the name of the Father..." He swept his free hand above her. "And the son, and the Holy Spirit..." Made the sign of the cross. "As Jesus rose, we too shall rise." Then he shoved Kimberly beneath the water.

Tehlor waited for her to breach. For Phillip to lift his hand and introduce the newest Haven initiate. But Daniel stepped around the back of the shock tank and leaned over, setting his hand on the woman's chest. Phillip gripped Kimberly's shoulder and trapped her. *Oh.* Tehlor held her breath, watching the water shift. At first, Kimberly made tiny, uncomfortable movements. Tapping her fingers. Lifting and lowering her legs. A minute went by. Kimberly gripped the sides of the trough before reaching outward, grappling for someone, anyone. After that, she flailed. Water splashed over the sides of the tank. Phillip held her under, enduring her wild arms, and Daniel braced, dodging desperate kicks.

A muted, waterlogged sound came and went, a shout or plea, before Kimberly went still.

Someone gasped. Another person whispered, "The Lord will keep her."

Everything inside Tehlor said *get the fuck out* and *run* and *this is not what we prepared for*, but she locked her knees and kept her expression neutral. *Don't freak out, don't freak out, don't—*

Amy manhandled Sophia toward the edge of the trough and grabbed the girl's wrist, forcing her closer. Sophia growled and tried to yank away, but a brittle hush made her wince. She relented, allowing Amy to guide her open palm into the water.

"The Lord will keep her!" Phillip shouted.

The congregation followed. "The Lord will keep her!"

Black tendrils snaked across Sophia's eyes, diving into her pupils. In a rush, her wide gaze turned black as night. Her head snapped backward, and her mouth peeled open. The lace collar framing her jaw trembled under the weight of a silent scream, but the sound still ricocheted inside Tehlor's head. She heard it—Sophia's guttural howl mingling with a thousand unrecognizable voices—and squeezed her eyes shut. Noises filtered through. Bones, chewed. Wings, beating. Eagles, shrieking. Teeth, gritted. When she cracked her eyes open again,

Sophia's bottom jaw had stretched low enough to hint at breakage. Wind whipped through the gazebos, causing lit wicks to quiver.

Kimberly shot forward, spitting up a lungful of water, and the Haven congregation erupted into applause. Shouting, prayer, and a chorus of *hallelujah* filled the air. Amy's broad smile dimpled her face. Phillip grinned triumphantly, hoisting Kimberly out of the trough. The freshly baptized woman steadied herself. She stood, sopping wet, and glared at the ground, hollow-eyed—*different*. Rose nodded, her smile brutal and cold, and shifted her attention to Tehlor.

"Thought so," Lincoln breathed out.

Tehlor reached into her purse and cupped her shaky hand around Gunnhild.

"Holy mother, you will carry Haven's light," Phillip said, wrapping a fresh towel around the shell of the woman he'd drowned moments prior. "The Lord blesses those who are obedient, for the devout find themselves in the presence of miracles!"

Creeping sickness spread through Tehlor, turning her stomach. *Mother. Carry. Miracles.*

She choked. "He's... These women are—"

"I know," Lincoln said.

"You don't," she snapped under her breath, shifting her wide eyes to him. He couldn't. Not really, not entirely, not truly. "You don't," she said again, softer, harsher.

Lincoln nodded and squeezed her hand.

The dead can't say no. Tehlor swallowed hard. Did they really think it would work, though? Did Phillip and Rose actually believe they could sire children with... She stared at Kimberly—at what was left of her—until her stomach roiled again. She switched her attention to the De'voreaux sisters.

Sophia stumbled. Before she could fall, Amy tugged her upright. Blood streamed from Sophia's nostril and darkened her earlobe. It welled in her nailbeds and pooled in the grooves between her pearly teeth. All magic came with a cost, but whatever slithered around inside Sophia wreaked havoc on her body. It took from her. It stole.

"It's killing her," Tehlor said, glancing at Lincoln.

"Yeah, but I'm pretty sure they know that already," he said, exhaling a short, sharp breath. "Necromancy sure is a hell of a miracle, though. Who needs a pamphlet when fifty people saw that shit with their own eyes."

"Think she's the finale?"

He nodded, plastering on a grin for the crowd. "Most likely."

"The lady they pulled out of the bucket is a fuckin' shell, Lincoln—"

"I know."

"Okay, but—"

"Tehlor Nilsen," Rose exclaimed, beckoning the pair with an outstretched hand. "Come and be reborn!"

The churchgoers whooped and clapped. Someone touched Tehlor's arm, stroking her like a cat. Another person whispered a prayer, something about Genesis, and a man swatted Lincoln on the back, congratulating him. When Lincoln stepped forward, she stayed anchored in place. It took another gentle nudge before she finally crept through the crowd.

Everything is fine. Think. Think. She took measured steps, buying time. *Don't freak out. Don't give yourself away.* She searched Kimberly's reanimated corpse for signs of true life. Stared at her wet, pale skin, and tried to meet her desolate gaze, but there was nothing. The woman's chest did not move. She did not blink, breathe, or speak. Kimberly was gone and whatever stood next to Daniel, swaying back and forth on unsteady legs, was a lifeless marionette. *A corpse can't carry a fucking child.* She saw the hunger in Rose's eyes, the delirium in Phillip's grin. Regardless of the truth, plausibility, ethics, right and wrong, and whether the Breath of Judas gave them access to the next generation of Haven soldiers or not, Rose and Philip had established control. In the eyes of their congregation, they were as close to God as someone could get.

Remember to smile. Tehlor took her place at Lincoln's side. *Don't give in; don't let them see you afraid.* She resisted flinching when Rose took her by the shoulders and slid her hand beneath the strap of her purse, easing it away. *Gunnhild*, she thought, desperately. She tried to smile, to be approachable, to use her wits, to think on her feet. *What now, what next, what do we do, what do we do, what—*

"And you, son of Adam, will assist in her baptism," Phillip said. He dipped his thumb in a bowl of perfumed oil and made the sign of the cross on Lincoln's forehead. "Anointed one, will you see her through to a life anew?"

Lincoln lifted his brows. He shot Tehlor a careful glance and nodded. "I will."

"Tehlor," Phillip prompted, waving toward the shock tank.

Don't crack. She steadied her uneven breath and took off her coat, draping it over a fold-out chair before she stepped into the cool water. *Don't break.* It soaked her to the bone. Her jumpsuit clung to her. *How do we get out?* She stared at the roof of the gazebo. Watched a breeze rattle the unlit jar-lights. *Tell me what to do*, she chanted, reaching for magic, for Fenrir, for Hel, for anything, anyone. *I am a child of old*, she pleaded. Water licked her cheeks. *Daughter of Freya, keeper of ancient rites, blood of the betrayed. Hear me. Hear me. I beg of thee.* She exhaled and turned, meeting Sophia's onyx eyes. *I beg of thee.*

Lincoln slipped his hand into the water and placed his palm on her sternum.

Rose came to stand beside the trough. She traced the willow cutting tucked behind Tehlor's ear. "Will you return clean and pure, sister in Christ?" She touched the red ink on Tehlor's throat the same way a wasp might perch on bare flesh. "Will you become a vessel? Will you kneel before the Lord?"

Fenrir's voice boomed through her skull. *The mighty kneel before no one.*

Rage lit inside her, singeing the tail-end of her misplaced fear.

"You were right," Tehlor whispered. She met Lincoln's two-toned eyes and gave a curt nod. "Your plan was better."

Rose cocked her head, confused.

A handsome, raspy laugh rumbled behind Lincoln's closed lips.

Tehlor reached into her boot, gripped the leather handle, and pulled her hidden hunting knife free. She swung, jamming the blade beneath Rose's ear. A guttural, wet noise lurched from the Haven matriarch. Her eyes bulged, cemented on Tehlor, and her pink mouth dropped open. She coughed and sputtered. Like Kimberly, she pawed at the air, unable to properly defend herself. Tehlor twisted the knife and opened Rose's throat.

Blood gushed over Tehlor's knuckles and dripped into the baptism trough, splattering her cheeks. She wrenched the weapon free. *There, bitch. Go shake hands with Christ.* Rose crumbled into a lifeless heap beside the shock tank.

No one moved. No one screamed. People watched, waiting for another miracle. Their saucer-eyes searched for a signal, for reason, but no one said *amen*, no one prompted them to holler or speak in tongues, no one praised God or quoted scripture. All was quiet except for Tehlor's harsh breath and the sound of water sloshing over the sides of the trough as Lincoln lifted her out.

Phillip whimpered and took a half-step backward, staring at his dead wife. He lifted his arm and jabbed at Tehlor and Lincoln. Despite his shaking arm, blown pupils, and sheet-white face, he didn't make a sound. Couldn't, probably. He gaped, transferring his shocked gaze from Rose to Tehlor.

What a sad, sorry thing to watch a murder take place and expect an absent god to intervene.

Tehlor turned the knife over in her hand. Frost pushed through her wet clothes, but the angry, frantic magic stirring beneath her skin coaxed heat to unfurl in her core. Steam rose from her jumpsuit. She reached for the band holding her bun in place and pulled, allowing her damp hair to tumble over her shoulders. *Be with me,* she begged and snatched at the energy tethering her soul to Lincoln's. *Be with us.*

"The Lord will keep her," Tehlor muttered. She spat on the ground and crouched beside Rose's corpse, plastering her palm over the leaking wound. Carefully, with intent, she smeared sacrificial blood across her face. *Hear me.* "Fenrir, be kind," she whispered. Her small palm fit neatly around the handle of the knife. Blood clumped in her eyelashes. "I come to you humble and wanting, great wolf, for I am a child of the true gods, and I wish to carry their glory into the new world."

Finally, Phillip let out a horrified scream.

Daniel reached for his holstered firearm.

In a sudden whip of frozen wind, the candles died, and the revival devolved into chaos.

Magic surged. Tehlor inhaled raggedly and got to her feet, whipping toward Lincoln. His energy pulled tight around her own, shackled to her skeleton like a second self. Same as in her dream, she felt the mountainous presence of Fenrir standing above her, teeth bared, calling her *chainbreaker*. Parishioners shouted. Someone shrieked and bellowed, yelling for police, for help, for an ambulance. The voices—so near, so close—became distant and muffled. *Focus*. But Tehlor was no longer in control. Not completely. She was Lincoln, and he was her. She was Fenrir, and Hel, and Loki, and Magni. She was every voice in the Æsir. She sparked, set ablaze by demon kings, scorched by the sorcery that'd followed Lincoln out of hell.

Fenrir's voice rode the back of a wintery gust. "Rise."

Tehlor sucked in a great breath and felt her body pull toward the sky. She was weightless and buoyant, channeling a storm as Haven broke apart. Energy swept upward from the bloody body at her feet. She gasped again, catching her breath, and saw herself through Lincoln's gaze—eyes milky white, palms open, feet hovering above the ground—and felt his heart squeeze and sputter.

Be vigilant.

When she reached for life, she found it, and when she gripped, twisted, snapped, it went to pieces in her hands. Her knuckles buckled inward. The knife dropped, sinking into the snow beneath her boots. A gunshot rang out. She only caught a flash, the barely-there outline of a threat, and heard the buzz of a bullet whizz past her. *Daniel*. Another shot came and went, aimed at Lincoln. The bullet grazed his arm. *Pain*. Sudden; minuscule. Tehlor did not need to turn toward him, or look at him, or aim. Her power—Fenrir's power—lashed out and struck Daniel's sternum. The man's ribcage caved. Bone, splintered, punctured, bent outward, curving like antlers from his gaping chest.

It was not her hands doing the breaking, but it was. It was not her mind manipulating hot marrow, but it was. It was not her magic peeling back flesh, but it was.

Lincoln's animal growl filled the air, and in her peripheral, where their magic blurred and broke, she saw his wolfish maw slicked red, his

teeth snapping at soft jugulars, his human hands squeezing and twist-
ing. He snatched Phillip, searing each side of the pastor's face with
steaming palms, and snapped his neck. When the Haven patriarch fell,
his cheeks wore charred flesh, as if Lincoln had pushed hellfire into his
skin.

Völva imbued with Vanir. The voice snaked through her, familiar
and not. *We are alike, you and I.*

Tehlor tried to find the source, but her limbs were locked, her body
suspended, held by godkin.

I know you, she wanted to scream, remembering Sophia's fingers
curved around the bottom of a locked door. *Jesus wept, you fuckin'
coward.*

The sound of carnage faded, replaced by crashing waves, arctic
wind, battle drums, and clashing steel, and Tehlor Nilsen could not
separate herself from the woman the gods had decided she would be.
Right then, she became a vessel for violence, shattering bodies with a
single thought, stripping lifeforce with a sweep of her hand, coaxing
blood from mouths, eyes, and ears as she pleased.

But when Hel whispered, "Be glad," Tehlor recognized pain.

Not the pain of another. Not being grazed by a bullet, not being
kicked, not being slapped, not being clawed, or shoved, or swatted.
Disruptive pain. *True* pain.

No, she thought, *no, no, no.* But reality tunneled inward, cutting
through the sound of drums.

All at once, Tehlor's vision cleared.

Amy stood in front of her, wide-eyed and red-cheeked, choking on
ugly sobs, holding the hilt of Tehlor's fallen knife against her belly.
The blade buried deep. Searing pain jostled Tehlor into the present.
Godkin, gone. Power, gone. Magic, gone.

Even the faithful face betrayal.

Tehlor Nilsen, chosen by Fenrir, blessed by Hel, had underestimated Amy De'voreaux.

"It was a prophecy," Tehlor whispered. Copper tainted her tongue.

Amy sniffled and let the knife go, gripping Tehlor's face with both hands. "I can still save you. I can fix this, I can—I can make this right. We'll be gorgeous mothers, Tehlor." Blood seeped through Tehlor's jumpsuit, down her thigh, tickling her knee. *Damn*, Tehlor thought, choking on an ugly sob, and then, *Lincoln*. Amy continued, crazed. "We'll be *holy* mothers. Birth blooming from death. Beautiful, right? I promise—it's not too late, it's never too late, I can—"

Her soupy babbling was shredded by a scream. Fingertips raked Tehlor's cheeks and Amy fell, pulled into the snow by a living corpse.

Kimberly, or whatever she'd turned into, clawed at Amy's body. Ripped at clothes, then flesh, and dove fist-first into her stomach. Amy's ghoulish wail echoed through the preserve, accompanied by a slippery *crunch*. Kimberly pulled and plucked, emptying Amy's body of muscle and organs. It was a quick, awful death, barbaric and fitting.

Tehlor clumsily felt across her stomach and wrapped a shaky hand around the knife.

Lincoln. The quiet scared her. *Lincoln, Lincoln, Lincoln. You're here, I know you're here, you have to be here, you didn't leave me, you wouldn't leave me, don't leave me—*

"*Shit*," Lincoln barked, turning her roughly.

"You didn't leave," she said, bewildered.

Blood speckled his sweater and coated his hands. His mouth dripped crimson.

Beautiful beast, she thought. *Still mine.*

"Leave? *What?* Look, don't..." He exhaled through a frustrated growl and reached timidly for the knife. "This'll hurt like a bitch, okay? Just stay still. I can..." He inhaled through his nose and narrowed his eyes. "I can heal you, but this has to come out first."

As he wrapped his hand around the hilt of the knife, she realized she'd never seen him afraid before. She laughed, one single *hah*, and cried out when he pulled the blade free. He yelped, too, and plastered his palm over his stomach, concealing a matching wound.

Tehlor's knees buckled. She swayed into him, but Lincoln did not let her fall.

"Where's my rat," she mumbled.

The darkness thickened. She heard Lincoln's heartbeat, pounding, dwindling.

Lincoln cradled her in his lap, fumbling for the knife, muttering something in a language she didn't know. Latin. Aramaic, maybe. Demon-speak.

"Where's my rat," she said again, louder.

"In my fucking pocket," he snapped. "Can you stay still? Jesus Christ, Tehlor. You..." He blew out an annoyed breath, rolled his sleeve to his elbow, and picked up the knife, setting the blade against his forearm. "You went nuclear, you know that? Old-world shit."

She snorted, staring at his perked ears, pretty snout, and stern eyes. Her vision doubled, tripled. She clung to *here* and *now*, to *then* and *there*, coughing through labored breath.

"Breathe," Lincoln said. His two-toned eyes glinted.

Lincoln flattened his palm over the puncture.

"You first," she said, glancing at his leaking stomach.

Lincoln ignored her.

"*You first*," she hollered, choking on coppery ichor.

Lincoln hushed her. She didn't hear what else he said, couldn't parse the incantation tumbling past his sharp teeth, but she felt her flesh catch fire.

As wicked heat chewed her skin, cauterizing the wound, Tehlor threw her head back. She screeched, digging her heels into the bloody snow, and fisted her weak hands in Lincoln's shirt. Before her mind clicked off, consciousness shooed by immeasurable pain, she caught a glimpse of Sophia De'voreaux crouched in the darkness, hand poised like a puppeteer, staring back at her.

Chapter Twelve

CHURCH MASSACRE IN WILDERNESS PRESERVE
INVESTIGATED AS MURDER-SUICIDE

The headline scrolled past the bottom of the muted flatscreen.

Seven days ago, enthusiastic news anchors had reported on a brutal incident in the Gideon backcountry. The local sheriff refused to name suspects, and the investigation was under lock and key, but Tehlor still tuned in every morning, waiting for her picture to appear, for the headline to change: *Local woman identified as prime suspect in Haven slaughter.* She shifted on the couch, laid out in an unfamiliar place with her shirt bundled beneath her armpits, flinching as Lincoln peeled a bandage off her stomach.

"It's getting better," he said, tipping his head to inspect her charred skin.

A blackened handprint replaced the nasty gash. For seven days, she'd limped around, hissing and complaining, begging Freya for mercy, and for seven days, her ruined flesh sizzled with every breath. He was right, though. It was happening slowly, but hellfire be damned, she was healing.

The house on Staghorn Way was not home, but they'd needed shelter after the revival, and staying at her townhouse had been too risky. Somehow, they'd circled back to their origin, waiting for the person they'd mutually betrayed to walk through the front door again. She tracked slow-falling snow through the window while Lincoln dabbed at the burn with a damp cloth, and tried not to flinch when he applied a cooling ointment. She'd mashed the salve together herself, imbuing it with blessings and hope. *Do not leave me*, she'd whispered to each herb, imagining godkin poised on the beach in her dream, *do not forsake me*. Each night, she envisioned the preserve—candles, prayer, bloodshed—and each night, she found another missing piece, collected another lost memory.

Lincoln, carrying her into the townhouse, hoisting her into the bathtub, holding her face between his reddened hands. *Don't you fuckin' dare, Tehlor. Look at me, c'mon, hey!* Something shattering, footsteps hurrying, voices carrying. *Listen, kid, I saw what you can do, okay? Bring her back. Do it, or I'll*—Sophia De'voreaux's blotchy face. How badly Tehlor had wanted to say *I'm still alive, I'm still here*, and how impossible that simple action had been. Sophia, stitching Tehlor's flighty soul into place. Agony, agony, agony. Lincoln, standing in the doorway, holding the matching wound on his stomach with one hand and swatting at a stubborn tear with the other. And before that—*before, before*—how the night had turned vicious, and she had, too. Lincoln, lifting a man by the throat. Bodies bending backward, breaking. Death, how it sounded, how it smelled. How life sputtered out in her palm. Amy's arm loosed from the socket. Her eyes gouged, her teeth cracked—

"Hey." Lincoln finished taping a new bandage over the hand-print—*his* handprint—and brushed his knuckles across her cheek. "You good?"

Tehlor chewed her bottom lip. "Tired."

They hadn't talked about it. Not extensively, at least.

The night she'd become death, met death, escaped death, Tehlor had startled awake, confused and terrified, reaching for Lincoln. He'd fumbled for her quaky hands. Made a sound shaped like severe relief. Kissed her desperately.

She was alive, Haven was destroyed, and Lincoln hadn't left.

Fuckin' hell.

Nothing else mattered, really.

She pushed her shirt into place and sat up, grimacing.

"I made Sophia some toast earlier, but she won't come down," he said.

Tehlor remembered Sophia slinking through the doorway after she'd lurched into Lincoln's arms. Remembered pitch-black eyes, gnashing teeth, how an hour before that, the strange, magically com-promised girl had pierced through Fenrir's shield and managed to enter Tehlor's mind. *Powerful little thing*. Fear paralyzed her, but she swallowed and steeled her expression.

"Fair. I wouldn't come down either if..." She gestured between herself and Lincoln. "We were waiting."

Lincoln sat on the edge of the coffee table. Sometimes when she looked at him, she saw blood where there wasn't any. Flashbacks from the revival came and went, snapping around her heart like a beartrap. For seven days, she'd avoided her reflection, afraid Rose Whitman might look back at her. She glanced away, focusing on a ritual candle melting on the windowsill. She'd etched runes into the wax and prayed for flowers on her bed again. But the candle burned, and the house slumbered, and her gods did not grant another audience.

"Maybe you should talk to her."

Tehlor stood, bracing on the armrest, then the back of the couch. She glanced at the ceiling. "I'll give her another day."

"We might not *have* another day," he said, sighing.

Gunnhild squeaked. She climbed out of the snuggle ball tucked against the corner of the couch and hopped over to Tehlor, asking to be held.

A car door opened and closed. Another did, too. Ice crunched under weighty steps. Shoes made hollow, hoof-life sounds on the sturdy, renovated porch.

Tehlor placed Gunnhild on her shoulder and inhaled a long, deep breath. Her lungs tightened. She glanced at Lincoln and lifted a brow, shifting her jaw back and forth.

The lock twisted. Afternoon light streamed into the foyer followed by a dusting of fresh snow.

"Welcome home," Tehlor said.

Colin Hart paused mid-unlace of one polished Oxford. Shadows purpled the thin skin beneath his sunken eyes, and a bruise marred the angelic ink creeping above his collar. Whatever he'd been dealing with, it looked exhausting. He tilted his head, inquisitive gaze flicking around the quiet house. Tehlor stepped into view, leaning her shoulder against the closed closet.

"Oh, hey. What're you..." Colin's question disintegrated.

Lincoln followed Tehlor's lead, walking around the back of the couch to stand at the end of the hall. He leaned against the kitchen table with his thumbs curled through his beltloops, chin held high, staring at Colin down the slope of his human nose.

Bishop shouldered through the front door and dropped their backpack. Snow clung to their denim coat, and they plucked their glasses off to clean the lenses with their sleeve, shooting Colin a tired, confused smile.

"What..." They slid their glasses back on and followed Colin's harsh gaze.

The moment Bishop Martínez laid their eyes on Lincoln Stone the air turned electric. Their pupils stretched into diamonds. They reached into their waistband and drew a sleek, black pistol, swinging the weapon forward without pause. They held the gun firmly, chest-high, and stepped in front of Colin.

"Be for real," Tehlor barked. She rolled her eyes and scratched the top of Gunnhild's head.

Above them, hinges creaked. The landing at the top of the staircase wheezed beneath cautious footsteps. Once again, the house on Staghorn Way began to tremble.

Bishop did not lower the gun. Colin held his breath. Behind her, Lincoln hummed, soft and thoughtful.

Great, she thought. *Here we go.*

Tehlor sighed. "We've got bigger problems, brujo."

RETURN TO GIDEON

SAINT
SORROW
SINNER

ACKNOWLEDGEMENTS

Wolf, Willow, Witch was a stubborn exercise in reflection. This little book became a personal healing journey for me. It's the result of a headstrong need to explore womanhood, gender, and sexuality in a raw, inelegant format. I hope the people who needed Tehlor found strength in her graceless determination and solace in her ruthless self-examination. She is all of us, I think, in one way or another.

Thank you to my peers and mentors—D.C., Aveda, Em, Jo, Koren, Rien (both of you), Kellen, Mo, Jen (both of you), Rafael, Harley, R.M., Iris, Foxglove, Lily, and so, so many others. Thank you, Bethany, for being my industry champion. Thank you to my loyal readers for supporting my work. Thank you to the queer creators who pour love into their craft even in the darkest hours: you make work like mine feel possible. Your perseverance catches fire in me constantly.

Thank you to my family, always. Thank you to the friends who walk through life with me—Mané, my fast girl, and Nathan, my gentle giant, and Ev, my curious adventurer, and Tasha, my beautiful sister, and Maureen, my wise mystic—and hold space for me, mess and all. As always, you keep me in my power when I can't seem to conjure it on my own. I am blessed to have you.

About ☽

Freydís Moon (they/él/ella) is a bestselling, award-winning author, tarot reader, and Pushcart Prize nominee. When they aren't writing or divining, Freydís is usually trying their hand at a recommended recipe, practicing a new language, or browsing their local bookstore. You can find their poetry, short stories, and fiction in many places, including *Strange Horizons*, *The Deadlands*, and elsewhere.

https://freydismoon.carrd.co

For information about the cover artist and interior illustrator, please find **M.E. Morgan** here: https://morlevart.com/

Printed in Great Britain
by Amazon